IS ORION HOME?

Is Orion Home?

P. I. ADAMS

First published in 2004 by
Serendipity,
Suite 530,
37 Store Street,
Bloomsbury,
London, WCIE 7QF

British Library Cataloguing-in-Publication data
A catalogue record for this book is available from the British Library

ISBN 1 84394 091 4

Printed and bound in the UK by Alden Press, Oxford

This book is dedicated to my wife Marjorie, without her inspiration it would not have been written.

One night Marjorie said if I was not interested in the television, to go on my computer and write my own stories. That inspired me to write my collection of short stories, then this novel.

With fond memories,
My Love For Ever.
Phil.

To my sons Steve and Robert for their encouragement, for the enthusiasm of my friends of fifty years Jean and Haydon Brown, and The Withernsea Writers' Group. To Audrey Dunne who has written many books of her own; you taught me and others how to lay out a story, I hope I have done you proud.

Contents

Foreword

Where does a thing begin? Phil Adams was a member of the Creative Writing Workshops I had been asked to organise by Theatre Productions, that was a fact, but the workshops weren't the beginning of the book. Averil Coult and Sara Hawkins, who *are* Theatre Productions were producing a Community Play in Withernsea. The lively group of writers in the workshop were enthusiastically involved in it. Eventually, after much hard work and fun, the play became *The Holderness Saga*. It had a cast of eighty-four people (not all of them in my workshop). Phil played nine parts.

So, in a way, the book began there, as part of this vast event in Withernsea – a seaside town standing between the North Sea and the mystical Plain of Holderness, edged, at Spurn Point, some two miles, away by the wide estuary of the River Humber. Numerous workshops and events were arranged preceding the play, and many people were encouraged, as perhaps they had never been encouraged before, to explore their talents, believe in themselves and find confidence.

Phil was very much a part of this. I remember in the writing workshop his enthusiasm. There was an aura of excitement. Something was afoot and everyone was excited. In the beginning it was Phil's autobiographical writing I found fascinating. It centred around his unusual childhood in Wales, a childhood that seemed free and uninhibited. His language, still echoing very individual turns of phrase from those days, was vivid, colourful and full of feeling. His family too were keen for him to record their ancestral anecdotes. Phil, however, had other ideas.

His passion was to write a science fiction novel interwoven

with a love story. This desire became more urgent one evening during a group exercise. I wanted to illustrate the ease with which chapters for a book can be planned; that it is like playing a game. The group decided on a book of science fiction. We gave it the title *Worlds Apart*. Thumbnail notes for chapters began to emerge. Phil was interested. He suggested *Jane Meets a Stranger* for chapter three. The next week he had written up the whole episode, some of which became part of *Is Orion Home?* where Jane, in the event, became Jean. The *Withernsea Writers' Group* was formed as a follow-up to my course and Phil set to work producing more writing. By now he was thoroughly smitten with the task.

This breakthrough, however, was not the beginning of Phil's ambition to write a work of science fiction. The germ of the idea first presented itself in 1946, when he was on military service in the Middle East. The pyramids of Egypt filled him with awe. The sheer size of the blocks of stone and the accuracy of the shapes set his imagination going. Surely there was no modern equipment that could ever make such impressive structures. He felt that this vast process must have been carried out by a more advanced culture than any we could match.

Back home again in England he could not forget the pyramids. He began to search library archives for information. But nothing he found could equal the impression he had received on first seeing them himself. The theories of how these monuments came into being were disappointing. How were they built, and why? Again, he went back to his earlier thoughts. What if the earth had been dominated by four major races: Indian, Chinese, African and European, on four different continents? And what if one race had been the earth's original inhabitants, and the others came from somewhere else; from outer space? The pyramids, he discovered, are perfectly aligned to the stars in Orion's belt. What more proof did he need?

It was, Phil always thought, a privilege to have been in the Middle East, especially Egypt where he was so inspired by the pyramids. The lifelong intrigue and sense of wonder he found there has its fulfilment in this book. And who knows, but that *Is Orion Home?* is yet another beginning, one that originated millennia ago in the shadow of the pyramids, or on another planet in the mind of beings of a different kind?

Audrey Dunne
2nd December 2003

CHAPTER I

The Discovery

'Come on Paul, it was your idea to come walking on the dales. We have still have about two miles to go before we get to the hotel, what was it you said? "Dave, I have a great idea to celebrate your twenty-first. Let's go for a walk across the dales, it will be something you will always remember", so come on get a move on. Another thing, I still think we should have kept to the route marked on the map.'

'Can it Dave, and let's have a five minute break. I need one, I'm older than you.'

'Ha, you poor old thing. I forgot, what is it now, seven months and two days older than me? I guess we had better stop for a rest, but only for a few minutes.'

While Paul sat down and had a drink from his flask, Dave went on up to the top of the rise they had been climbing to have a look at what was up ahead. After having had a good look around he came back to sit with Paul.

'There is a deep gully up ahead and it is going in our direction. There are trees in it so we can have some shade for a while, this sun is getting hot. Come on, the sooner we get to the hotel the sooner you can put your feet up, have that nice pint of cool beer.'

'OK, now you are you are talking my language. Where is that gully?'

It wasn't long before they were in the gully, thankful for the shade. After they had been walking for about half an hour, they noticed that the gully was getting deeper and full of brambles. Looking around them Dave said, 'I think it is time we got out of here, let's climb out before we get stuck in those brambles. Damn, we will have to go back until we can find a place to climb out.'

They retraced their steps for about fifty yards.

'There. Look, Dave at that tree sticking out of the bank. If you gave me a lift up I can pull you up from that branch, then we should be able to reach the top.'

Standing below the branch, Dave put his hands together. Paul placed his foot in them, reached up and grabbed the branch. Then he heaved himself up and sitting astride he reached down and grasped Dave's hand then pulled. As Dave put his full weight on the branch, the whole tree, roots and all came away from the bank taking them both with it as it crashed down into the gully. Dave looked up from a tangle of branches. 'That was a clever idea I don't think. What are you trying to do, kill us both?'

Climbing out of the tangle of branches, Paul looked up to where the tree had come away from the bank.

'Dave what do you make of that up there? It looks like a sheet of metal behind where the tree roots were.'

Dave was already scampering up the tree trunk to see what it was. Paul shouted, 'Wait for me.'

Reaching the top and looking though the tree roots they saw a rounded sheet of polished metal; Paul looked at Dave.

'What do you think? Is it a bomb?'

They looked at one another. Dave put out his hand and gently touched it.

'It can't be a bomb, it looks too new. Let's see if we can move the earth away from it and have a better look.'

Carefully they moved the earth away from the sides of it, then they saw that it appeared to be a cylinder about 2 feet long and 10 inches wide. Eagerly they pulled away more earth, then it started to move. Before they had time to do anything it crashed to the bottom of the gully and rolled to a stop. They both dropped back down into the gully and stood there looking at it. Paul got down on his knees and put his ear to it, looking up at Dave.

'Thank God for that. It's not ticking, I don't think it's a bomb.'

Paul lifted the cylinder up and was surprised to find it was a lot lighter than he had expected.

'Come on Dave, we'll take it to the hotel with us, then decide what we are going to do with it.'

'I don't know, I think we should leave it here and tell the police or someone about it. What if it is a bomb or something dangerous?'

Meanwhile Paul had been moving his hand up and down the cylinder feeling for any cracks to see if it could be opened. Suddenly he jumped back letting out a yell.

'What's happening?'

The cylinder had started to open along almost its full length. They both just sat there looking at it as the top half opened and rested on the other side; there were more surprises, it was full of knobs and buttons. Dave gently put a finger on what appeared to be a mirror. Again the unexpected happened, a disc about 8 inches round rose up from the centre of the cylinder. Then, without having touched anything, a figure of a man appeared as a hologram. They watched as he pointed down at an identical cylinder in front of himself. Then moving his hand he picked up an object, put it on his head like earphones then appeared to point at them.

Then other objects kept appearing quickly with the man. Paul looked at Dave. 'In for a penny in for a pound.'

Picking up the earphones he put them on his head and as he did so the figure on the disc pointed to his mouth and started to speak.

Dave who was sharing the earphones with Paul said, 'What language is that? Do you recognise it? I don't.'

Then they noticed that the figure was pointing at them, then back at his mouth still talking.

'What do you think that all means Dave? He's miming with

his hands now as if he wants us to keep talking. That's it, look there is a table in front, he is pointing to something, what is it? It's a book and he's pointing to each object as they appear and naming them.' The holographic image had a globe of earth in front of him, then he spoke in English.

'My words should be in your language if the translator is working, I will point to different parts of the planet, and you can gave me your names for them. This will ensure we both know the parts we will be talking about.'

Suddenly the table vanished as he said, 'Can you say your alphabet, also your basic counting system?'

'Go on Dave; what about counting on our fingers?'

Dave already holding up one hand.

'Don't be daft Paul, it's a machine; how can it see what you are doing? But you could be on the right track; what about saying the alphabet like A for apple, B for book and so on. Use some of the things he showed us on the table, try it, and see what happens.'

'Good idea Dave, go ahead.'

After Dave had gone though the alphabet and numbers, there was silence for about a minute, and then the man on the screen was talking again.

'You may be wondering why this capsule opened so easily. Once your hand touched the capsule, it responded to the shape of your hand, the temperature and your pulse rate. These would indicate if you were human or non-human; it will only open to a human touch. If forced open it will fuse.

'The recorder will now be able to translate all I have to tell you about our past, hopefully your past also because you should be our descendants. There will be words and meanings that you may have to guess at.

'There is a black button, see where I am pointing, now let me explain about this recorder. If you want to switch it off for any reason press the yellow button, to carry on from where we left off press it twice. If you want to start from the beginning and close the lid, it can be reopened again by moving your hand from left to right. Press the black button twice, and it will restart from where you left off.

'My name is Joseph and I am from the central continent, the place you call Europe. We will go back to the globe and maps later in more detail, but in case something prevents me from finishing this we will proceed.'

The figure they now knew as Joseph moved to one side and sat down on a chair without legs.

'As you can see we have anti-gravity chairs. I point this out because it may be hundreds of years before your people will be advanced enough to have discovered this recorder. We will be leaving you all our technical knowledge in other capsules; which may help to rebuild our civilisation. They have been buried in the grounds of a library, that was still standing after the Ords had left. We believe that our world may revert to barbarism, and civilisation as we know it may be hundreds or thousands of years away. It maybe that your archaeologists will be the ones to find these capsules, this is one of our reasons for selecting the libraries.

'It is a scattered world now, and it will take many years to rebuild, but I know our people can do it. One thing our future civilisations must do is to worship one god and in one way. Religion is still the cause, or rather was the main cause, of strife between our races. It appears that our god is one and the same, but yet we somehow managed to think of him in slightly different ways, which created conflict between our races. Hopefully this will not be the case in your present world.'

The figure of Joseph moved to one side of the chair without legs.

'You may have anti-gravity again, and probably have chairs like the one I am using, if you do, you will also have all the other benefits of anti-gravity. Now I will recap our history from the time of the war with the Ords. They controlled the star systems in our part of the galaxy, not though by force, but by advancing our knowledge and understanding of each other's cultures, helping us to live in harmony with each other so that all wars and strife between the planets stopped. They advanced our technology so that the peoples all had good full lives.

'Firstly, up to 40,000 years ago or earlier their scout ships discovered this planet which was inhabited mainly by large animals, some of them dangerous. These were eliminated. They were already thinking of colonising this planet at some future time; it was only about 5,000 years before the catastrophe that we were brought here. At first, our race, the Iros, that you will have noticed is a white race, lived on the continent you have called Europe. Some 10,000 men and 10,000 females were landed on this middle continent, then the yellow-skinned race, the Jurmons - your Chinese - from the eastern continent, China. These were followed by the red race, the Mayas, or as you named them the Red Indians on the western continent.

'On our journey here we were in divided sections; a hundred in each. We had our meals there and were free to move around as we pleased; there were no guards that we could see, but we were watched. This we knew because we would be given instructions, when food was being prepared or if there was any disturbances, and when it was time for us to sleep we had to return to our seats. These would be inclined into sleeping positions and once we were in our seats we were enclosed in an energy field; this kept us in our own seating area.

'When the ship landed we were kept in our seats, until the complete side of the ship opened and we got the first sight of our new home. We were told that the guards would be leaving in the scout ship that had accompanied us. We were now on our own. There was equipment stored at the front and rear of the ship, and food for three months, after which we would have to find our own. A short time later we were released from our seats. Some got up jumping and shouting, some just sat as they were, others ran down the side of the ship, looking around them at their new home. They liked what they saw, trees and green swards of land.

'It was quite a while later that some of the men who had wandered around to the other side of the ship, came running back shouting, "There are women here, hundreds of them". There was a mad rush for everyone to see for themselves; this had been the thought in many of our minds, what would the reaction be with no women? No one had told us that there was an equal number transported with us.

'We began to pair off; not without some fights breaking out, as some of the men and women wanted to pair off with someone else. Having landed early in the day, it was noon before we began to organise ourselves into working parties.

'First a group searched the front of the ship. Here we found the robots, hundreds of them, and everyone cheered. When others found the anti-gravity sleighs in the rear, a great roar went up, couples were laughing and dancing. With food, tools, robots and anti-gravity sleighs, it was going to be just like home, so it was thought at the time.

'For the first week there was no order to anything, then men with vision and leadership began to organise. It took another week before there was some order, men and women were chosen as leaders for groups of five hundred couples, each group was given a share of the equipment and stores. Each group then sent out couples on sleighs to find their own space where they could set up their own community, build their own village.

'Within a month everyone left the ship's landing area. A thousand couples stayed to build our first town and the ship was stripped down to provide the basics for houses. While we organised the robots with the building, others used them to clear areas of land, sowing seeds of corn, and any other seeds they found. This was hit and miss, not knowing the seasons yet, but a start had to be made before the food ran out.

'There were animals around; some we saw others we heard, but we had no weapons and at this stage no one knew how to catch them or what to do with them if we did, hopefully we would find this information in the records left us.

'Luck was with us, there were some who recognised many of the fruits that grew close to our settlement. Once this was discovered we sent word to other groups, and they passed this onto their neighbours. As the years passed we built better towns and villages, learned to grow all the food we needed and our people began to move further afield. As populations increased we spread across the land you know as Europe.

'We began to explore further afield, going south where we discovered the southern continent you call Africa which was inhabited by a black race, a much younger one compared to us. These then were the original inhabitants of this planet and we later found other black men, on large islands far to the south. They were well established in their surroundings, living in mud huts. They were friendly, and good hunters using crude spears. They taught us how to hunt and how to cook the meats, this was how our ancestors would have been. At first they treated us as gods, mainly because we had come through the air on sleighs, we did convince them we were not. It was decided to let them develop in their own way, at their own pace as our ancestors had.

'Back in our own settlements we showed off our crude spears, demonstrating how to use them. It was not long before the men were making their own, then hunting parties went out to try their luck. They came back triumphant, but not without casualties; some had been injured with their own spears, others by the wild animals they were hunting, but we learned over time.

'As I have said, at first we had all remained in the one area but as time passed, groups of us set up our own villages, advancing further and further thoughout our land that you know as Europe. We had been left here by the Ords with some tools but no weapons. All the luxuries we had been used to were no longer available to us, we had to make our own and there were records left us on how to make just about anything, how to sow seed and plant crops. They had left us a variety of seeds with which to grow our own food, but had not shown us how to make robots or factories, these were things we would have to learn for ourselves. When we had got ourselves organised we realised that there were men and women with some degree of experience, or knowledge in making things. Although all manual work had been done by the robots, many men and women would do work as a hobby and many just watched the robots as they made things. This was now going to be very useful in the times ahead.

'Here I must explain why we had been brought here, from the Orion Belt. We were the malcontents of our planets, to the Ords we were the misfits, the troublemakers. Although all the different races from the various planets tolerated each other, there was always conflict, not actually war but often close to it. As we later learned, the Ords' plan was to put large groups of the three main humanoid races on one small planet. The hope was that it would prove we could, over time, learn to live together without conflict, to live in harmony with no discrimination of colour or creed. I will now show you the planet with the areas marked out where we had all been placed.'

Paul and Dave looked closely at the globe of the earth that had appeared. There was no Mediterranean Sea as they knew it, now showing just a narrow strip of water, more like a river than the sea. The poles looked to be at a different angle, and appeared to be in different positions.

'Look, that must be America where it says red race' said Dave. 'Mayas and Europe with the white race and over here in China the yellow race. So that is why there are four coloured races on this small planet, I have often wondered about that. The Mediterranean Sea looks smaller to me, and I cannot see the English channel, just inlets and lakes with narrow strips of land joining Britain and Europe. I suppose we will find out why later,' he added, pointing with his finger. 'Look, there are not as many islands, nor can I see Japan, it's all one continent.'

Paul answered with a nod of his head. While they were looking the scene changed back to figure of Joseph.

'Now that you know how we came to inhabit this lovely but small planet, I will tell you that it took us many years to build our great civilisation, with its beautiful cities. Although each race grew up with none or very little intermingling of races, there was no conflict like we had back on our own worlds. We developed fine commerce, and no one had more than he needed or less than he needed to enjoy life to the full. It had taken us nearly two thousand years of conflict and distrust before we finally learned to live in harmony. During the next five thousand years until the war with the Ords we built wonderful cities with graceful buildings, beautiful parks with lakes and woodlands filled with birds and animals for all to enjoy. Now we will visit some of our cities and what we have lost.'

The scene changed, and Dave and Paul could see they were now approaching a city, flying towards it over a lovely deep green belt of land.

'What is that Dave, it looks like a pyramid in the middle of the city? It's not like the ones we used to see in our books, they were brown, those are dazzling white, like polished marble.'

'Of course, they were coated with limestone, they look stunning like that. What a sight they would be in our time, and no buildings to block the view, only those parks in full bloom. There are two smaller ones behind them. I wonder if they are the Giza pyramids in Egypt, it looks like them.'

'You could be right Dave, except if they were in Egypt, they would be surrounded by sand.'

Joseph was talking again.

'As you can see, these pyramids are in the land you call Egypt. They have been completed, except for the stores which are been put in now. When the time comes the selected groups will enter, and stay in above ground level; most of them will stand or sit in the passage ways, we do not expect to be in them for long.'

'Well, would you believe it, he answered you.'

They were now looking down into a park, which was dotted with people in groups, some quite large, sitting, standing or walking, all laughing and enjoying themselves. There were craft of all sizes scattered about and the colours of the people's clothes made fascinating patterns on the green background. Dave wondered what Paul was thinking of it all, he would have to ask him later as there was no way that this moment could be disturbed.

They were approaching the city. It was like seeing a picture they had seen as young boys in a fairytale book, houses floating in the sky at different levels, others on the ground, some with spires, turrets, round and square. A lot of them appeared opaque, others all the soft colours of the rainbow, how they were built or what out of they didn't know, it could have been some kind of plastic. It was a city one dreams about, a fairy city, just like they used to see in fairy books as a young boy. 'What a world to live in,' thought Dave. 'Could we have something like this in years to come in our present world?' He would like to have thought so. There was also a lot of their transport flying in and out of the buildings. Most of them looked like glass bubbles. Some were small but most of them appeared to be four seats, they looked like half a bubble on platforms, Dave hoped they would get a better look at them later. Along wide avenues that looked like narrow parks, there were trees, some with masses of large flowers. People were sitting or walking along them, now and then a flyer would hover and pick someone up. Everyone looked happy but there were not as many children as one would have expected.

Now they were in one of the houses, a large room with floating chairs and sofas. There were two men and two women sitting around, talking and laughing not knowing that they were there. They could not hear them. 'More's the pity,' Dave thought. 'I would have liked to hear their voices.' They looked so happy, again they were in coloured clothes, the women wore a material so fine as to be almost transparent, showing off their beautiful bodies. The men were not so, but it was still possible to see well-proportioned bodies. Then appeared a boy and girl, the first they had seen close up. They skipped up to one of the couples and embraced them, laughing and gesturing, as though explaining something happy they had seen or done. Again they were beautiful, and wore what could be called pantaloons. The girl's were yellow with purple markings, the boy's were green of different shades.

After what only appeared to be minutes, the woman and the girl left the room, then the watchers saw them enter an open cubicle each. They both appeared to say something, the next thing their clothes just disappeared and both were standing there with no clothes on at all. They were enveloped in a mist, they both did a complete turn, and when the mist had gone, it could be seen they were saying something, and as if by magic the woman was dressed in blue and the girl in pink. Dave turned looking at Paul who just grinned back at him. Dave knew from that look that it was the first really nude woman he had seen. He looked back at the two of them as they walked back to join the others, and wondered if he would ever see anyone as beautiful again. 'Oh, dear I must keep my mind on this and not let it wander,' he thought.

Joseph was speaking again.

'We no longer had use for money which took away greed, the cause of most conflicts, and we had by now robots to fulfil most of our needs. They built our factories and grew our food, no one wanted for anything it was there for the taking. We had time to pursue whatever pastime we wished, go where we wanted even to the planets in our own solar system. We had the anti-gravity space ships that could take us to Mars, which was inhabited by the Kurups. These were a light-green skinned race and small in stature standing about 1.5 metres tall. With our gravity ships it would take us two days to get there. Having no wish to go beyond our solar system and arouse the interest of the Ords, we thought that by not infringing on their system or even appearing to be interested in doing so they would leave us alone. That was our big mistake. As we now know, they had been watching us with their robot-controlled ships from the time they put us here, but with the aim of suddenly destroying our world for no known reason. Many years ago we banned the development of any form of weapons on our planet, firstly to stop violence and wars among ourselves, and also to show the Ords we would not be, and never be a threat to them. We wanted to prove that we could all live in harmony together. This was the reason why we had been brought here in the first place by the Ords, as we had thought, but now we had to think again.

'We first learned of the Ords' intentions when a ship appeared from one of our own worlds, we were overjoyed to see twenty Chinese men disembark. After all the excitement had died down and we were starting to ask sensible questions, we heard the news we had never expected to hear. These men had found out where we were by accident when one them, who had been studying telepathy for many years with the aid of a machine, suddenly found he had succeeded beyond his wildest dreams. He could tune into the minds of the Ords without their knowledge and he kept this to himself until he accidentally tapped into a conversation between some Ords having a meeting. They were having a discussion about the discontented, the people they had sent to a small planet in a solar system on the edge of the galaxy, and how it had been decided by the inner council to eliminate them all. Why? "They never mentioned," said the man, "but we did learn that you were only 4.3 light years away and that it only took 23 days to get to this solar system using their magnetic line engines.

"For weeks we had listening to them, until finally we heard the news we had been waiting for, the co-ordinates for this system. We gathered together our friends here that we knew we could trust, Su Sang was the owner of this small ship that we came in. It was too slow if it was to make this journey in time to warn you, but with some clever dealing we managed to get a magnetic line converter installed, this enabled us to travel along the magnetic lines of force, it only took us 23 days to get here, as we discovered in time space travel, it worked out that represented one thousand years in earth time."

'That was not all the news they brought. On entering our system they had landed on Mars before coming to earth, where they had said that they would fight back if they were attacked. They believed that with their knowledge of weapons, their ability to reprogram their robots to develop and make new weapons, that they could safeguard their planet from any attack and they were willing to assist us with weapons should we need it. This information startled us; to make and use weapons to destroy life was against everything we believed in. It was decided to have a worldwide debate so that we could all have a say, whether to fight or find some other solution.

'We had all come from the Orion Belt where there are hundreds of planets, most of them inhabited by humanoids, others by some weird but highly intelligent creatures. Unfortunately it is the humanoid races that had the aggressiveness, which is why we three races were all put together on this small planet. We have developed a friendly understanding of each other's cultures and needs, but we are still not perfect. We have now come to accept that it is the nature of most humanoids, to have an inbuilt aggressive nature, even in the mildest of us.

'Within days the world committee had drafted out the details of the information we had been given, with three questions for everyone to answer and send to the central computer. Everyone had a computer either in their home, on their wrist or around their necks, so everyone could be contacted at the same time, and the following questions were sent worldwide.

These were:

1. Should we follow Mars and develop weapons and fight back?

2. Sue for a peaceful solution?

3. Prepare shelters against an attack in case they only sent their robots, in which case there would be no negotiations?

Within hours every family and home had received the information, within twelve hours all had been accessed by our computer. The majority were in favour of preparing shelters, but to also of trying negotiation. So we prepared for the worst and set about making shelters. Our plans were to build pyramids, which our scientists had worked out would be the best shape to deflect blasts or rays, so they were built in and around our cities, using our parks where necessary. The pyramids were to be used mainly for stores, such as communication equipment, anti-gravity devices, robots etc, also for our teachers, scientists and of course our leading committee members.

'In some of our parks, statues were made of many shapes and sizes, there were some that you called sphinx, these were large animals, in most cases lions. In the eastern lands of the planet, they made their statues as they saw the robots or the Ords. It became a fun pastime with them, making small ones for their homes. Some had gardens full of them, it was all good for keeping their spirits up and was encouraged.

'The first pyramids were not very successful, the shapes were not what we required nor would they do what they were intended for, they were not strong enough. The stones used were too small and, because of this many were left unfinished. Most of them were built by us in the place you called Egypt. Once we had found the right way to build them, we passed the information to the rest of the planet. Some copied them, others had their own ideas, and some who had no suitable rocks made them of other materials, all over the planet. Pyramids were built to align up to the same points of the compass since it had been predicted that the attack of the Ords would be from west to east. This was an accurate prediction, the Ords did attack from the west.

'The plan had been accepted readily throughout the planet, all our major cities and landmarks, had been positioned by set points of the compass. This had been done to assist spaceships from our solar system. It was a simple map to assist ships to their destination, the idea of aligning the pyramids the same way was readily accepted, although the reasons were different.

'Our main airport for space flight was in America. These were designated with large animals, or bird signs marked into the ground, to assist flights to land in the right loading or dispatching areas for other parts of the planet, they were going to or from. These signs could only be seen from the air.

'We decided to build our sphinx near the large pyramids; hopefully the Ords would think of them as more monuments, should any of their scout ships see them. It had been decided to make it appear that we had a planetwide craze to make sculptures. We selected an island you called Easter Island. There people made sculptures along the coast, giving the appearance of a competition. They all looked like large monstrosities but they appeared to have worked, because no notice was taken of the pyramids. The largest pyramid was built by the Mayas in a place named Peru, they had decided to use it to store food, clothing and robots for rebuilding the factories. The people mainly used the caves, and underground shelters, these were easy options for them.

'We decided to modify some of the robots to be able to use lasers to cut large blocks of stone, using anti-gravity platforms to transport them to our cities, or to the pyramid sites. Plans were sent out to every town and city with details of how to build them, and to keep them facing the same direction, which had been worked out as the most likely direction of attack by the Ord ships. In the northern part of Egypt, three pyramids were aligned to correspond to the position of our own worlds, in the Orion Belt, this was done to point out to future generations where our home worlds were, we are hopeful that there will be survivors to rebuild this world.

'It had been agreed to cover the pyramids with an extra protection against their rays, this was done by covering them with a polished layer of lime, which would help to deflect the rays. Unfortunately not everyone had our resources for lime blocks. Our scientists had worked out that the pyramid shape would be the most effective as a shelter against blasts and rays and as we now know, it worked very effectively. The air vents near the top of the pyramids would be sealed during any attack and we would use our own supply of oxygen. The vents were also aligned to our home worlds so we could contact them, should we be attacked by the Ords. Laser communicators were placed in position in the vents and lined up to our friends on our old homes; we wanted them to know what had happen should the worst occur.

'First the areas were marked out for each pyramid, then excavated to allow rooms to be built deep underground to give extra protection for the people, and food. The ground floor rooms were to be used to store equipment, the other rooms in the pyramids would be for equipment less likely to be harmed. Robots were programmed to do all the heavy work. For the cutting of the stone they used lasers, and could cut a block of stone square to a centimetre. The robots did the actual building and the laying out of the pyramids. These were transported on the anti-gravity platforms as some of the stones had to be transported great distances, across wide rivers and lakes.

'There were thousands of men and women involved in supervising the work, from the quarries to the building sites. It later transpired the pyramids were the saviour of mankind. Pyramids were built throughout the planet. There were some slight variations but the general shape was kept. In some parts they built mainly underground shelters, this was more so among the (Jurmons) Chinese whose cities were mainly along their coast.

'Our main problem was shelters for the rest of the population.

It was decided on a very simple idea, to dig long trenches, to cover them with large blocks of stone, then with soil at least two foot deep. With the blocks of stone this should prevent blasts and rays killing our people. Natural caves were be used where practical, cities were evacuated and the population sent into the country to use the trenches and caves as shelters. It was estimated that we had about fifteen years to prepare, which was very little time.

'We were as prepared as we could be in just fourteen and a half years, most of the equipment and goods that had to be stored in the pyramids was in place. It was a further nine months before the ships of the Ords came; during that nine months people were beginning to think it had all been a mistake, and the information had been wrong. If only that had been true! Many came back to their own homes, saying that they could get back in plenty of time if the Ords did attack, which many began to believe had been a misinterpretation of what had been overheard, and not a war against us. How wrong they were.

'When their ships came we tried to contact them but they did not reply to our pleading to talk, so it was assumed that they had only sent robots. The ships came across the Americas first. We were the next; they came in across the equator at us. The viewing recorders that had been set up on the ground and a thousand feet up right across the planet gave us a frightening view of the destruction that was happening. As they advanced on our city we watched as long lines of buildings just crumbled and vanished in a cloud dust. Buildings, trees, the houses that were still floating on their anti-gravity fields with the people still in them, all hoping that they would be safe up there, they just vanished like everything else and even the grass just disappeared. It was horrific, frightening beyond words, but we had to watch and wait to see if we would still be alive a few minutes from now. However to our relief the destructive rays passed over us, probably because of the pyramid shape and the heavy layer of lime that we had coated them with which helped to deflect the rays.

'Fortunately most of the pyramids survived intact. Not so the underground shelters, most of the people in them died because as the rays passed over or near them, the rays sucked up the oxygen. They were suffocated as they were, standing, sitting or laying down, as we discovered later from their mummified bodies.'

Joseph stopped speaking. Pressing the button to close it, Dave said, 'Wow, what do you make of that? Makes you think, can this be all true? Hell it is going to turn our history upside down. What are we going to do with it, take it to our hotel with us?'

'We will have to take it with us, there is a lot more to learn from it. Come on, it must be nearly lunch time and my belly thinks its throat is cut.'

They both laughed, but their eyes did not.

CHAPTER 2

The Girls

With Paul leading the way carrying the front end of the cylinder, it was not long before Dave said 'We will have to find some other way to carry it, the damn thing keeps slipping. Let's stop and think about it,'

Putting the cylinder down and looking around for inspiration, Paul said, 'It's simple, watch.'

Taking off his jacket and laying it on the ground, he rolled the cylinder onto it.

'You get hold of a sleeve and the bottom of the jacket like me. There, that's easier so come on.'

'Yes, but hold on, my backpack is slipping,'

Dave tightened the shoulder strap, then picking up his side of the jacket said, 'Let's go.'

When they entered the hotel they were lucky because there was no one in the reception area, except for the receptionist who was reading a book. They were signed in and given their room number in no time flat, not that they were going to complain because they were carrying the cylinder between them, so they quickly went up the stairs to their room. Once inside the room they put the cylinder under the bed just in case anyone other than themselves came in, then Dave ran to the bathroom.

'First one in gets to shower. You, my good man, can unpack the backpacks, don't forget I like my clothes put away neatly,'

'Yes Sir,' replied Paul with a laugh, 'But get a move on, I need a drink and something to eat.'

Within half an hour they were on their way to the dining room. Both looking refreshed and in clean clothes they entered, found an empty table by the window and sat down. Dave picked up the menu and studied it for a few minutes, then passed it to Paul.

'I'll have the steak with all the trimmings, do you want the same?'

'No, I am going to have the chicken for a change, and what about a glass of wine? Better still let's have a small bottle each, you will need a red with your steak and I need a white. OK with you?'

Dave was busy looking at the waitress across the other side of the room,

'Well just don't look, call her over for our order.'

With a big smile Dave raised his hand and he had hardly got his hand back down before she was standing over him, and giving Dave a smile to match his own.

'Yes Sir, what can I get you?'

'Go on Dave. Give the lady our order.'

Looking at Paul with a stare that could kill, and blushing like a young girl, Dave looked up at the smiling face of the waitress and stammered out the order. Then with a little skip she was gone.

They sat for a minute or two just pondering, then Dave said, 'What are we going to do about this thing we have found, are we going to report it to someone, and if so, who?'

'Right now all I am interested in is my dinner, I told you my stomach feels as if my throat has been cut so let's discuss it later. Ah, here it comes.'

The pretty young waitress was there beside them with a tray laden with their dinner, She carefully put Dave's in front of him giving him that come-on smile again, then placed Paul's down while still managing to look at Dave. Standing back, she murmured, 'I will be back with your wine in a moment Sirs.'

With that little skip she was away again but was back with the wine before they could put the first mouthful to their lips, saying, 'Shall I pour for you Sir?'

Blushing again Dave nodded. 'Yes please, I'll have the red.'

As she poured Paul's he said 'This looks great. I am going to enjoy this and what's for afters I wonder?' giving her a saucy smile and wink.

They both laughed and got on with their dinners.

Very little was said during the meal except for the occasional comment about how good it was. It was finished and the table cleared, Dave still giving the waitress the eye. Paul looked at him.

'If you can take your mind off that young lady we can discuss our problem.'

'There is no problem, I gave it a lot of thought while we were eating, I think we should see the video or whatever it is, all the way through before we tell anyone else about it. Once we do they would take it away from us, and we would never see it again. Besides, from what we have seen already, I'm not sure that the world is ready for it, and thinking about it we would be the first to learn the true history of the world. What we have seen and heard is breathtaking. Did you realise what was said about who the true original inhabitants of earth were, the black men from South America, Australia and Africa? That information alone is going to turn the world upside down. I don't think the world is ready for it, do you? Hell, it will rock the very foundations of civilisation. Yes, I reckon we already have a problem and we have only seen a part of it yet. What more are we going to learn from this thing, this recorder I think we had better call it? Is that OK with you?'

Without giving Paul a chance to answer, he continued 'What about those anti-gravity sleighs used to build the pyramids? I never could swallow that about thousands of slaves pulling those big blocks of stone with ropes, and over sand for hundreds of miles, I never could buy that.'

'To answer your question about what to call the thing, let's call it what it is, a time capsule. It can't be anything else can it?'

'Yes, of course not, you are right. It is a time capsule, our school buried one the year before I left. It was nothing like this one, we just put books, newspapers and photos and such like in it. That bit about them assuming that we still had those anti-gravity sleighs, and chairs, wish we had. What a difference they would make, there would be no need for roads, at least not as we know them at present. Just think, houses could be built on them and if you wanted to move anywhere in the world you could take it with you. Here's another thought for you. When the Europeans first discovered the black people they were primitives then, they were way behind us for hundreds of years. I guess that explains why, all the other races had thousands of years' civilisation on their home planets more than them. Good god, the world would be turned upside down, what the hell are we going to do?'

'Well thanks, I can get a word in at last. I thought you were never going to stop. Yes, I agree with you and there is more to come. I think we should find out what, before we turn the world upside down, as you said, it's giving me the willies thinking about it. Anyway let's forget about it for tonight, that waitress keeps looking over here giving you the eye, so, what are you going to do about it? Call her over and see if she has a friend for me; go on, then we can make a night of it.'

Dave looked over to her and gave her a signal to come over, the next second she was standing beside them giving Dave a smile to knock your socks off.

'Yes Sir, what would you like?'

'Firstly my friend here would like to know your name,' said Paul giving her an answering smile. 'My name is Paul and this odd-looking fellow is Dave.'

Without looking at Paul but fluttering her eyes at Dave she whispered 'Jean.'

Well Jean, what time do you finish work tonight? Maybe you can show us the nightlife here, and if you have a friend for me we can make a foursome, and hopefully all have some fun.'

In a quick whisper she said, 'I'll be right back.'

Going back to the kitchen, in a few minutes she was back saying, 'I finish in a few minutes, I've only got to clear a few more tables and I will be off duty, but my friend Kath finishes in another half a hour, that is her standing by the door.'

Turning his head to look where Jean was pointing with her little finger Paul saw a stunning little redhead giving him a wave.

At last Dave had found his voice, looking up at Jean. 'Where can we meet you both? How about in the bar here when you are ready. Is that OK?'

'Yes that will be fine, we will be as quick as we can.'

'Great. That will gave us time to go to our room and freshen up, so we will see you later.'

Looking a bit apprehensive she said, 'An hour's time, will that be alright?' giving Dave another big smile. Looking at Paul and nodding, he replied. 'That will be just fine, so an hour it is.'

Jean dashed off with her tray to finish clearing the tables. Dave with a twinkle in his eye said, 'You will have to watch yourself with Kath, she looks a right saucy one. Do you think you can handle her?'

Paul laughed. 'I will have a good try. Come on finish your drink and let's go to our room and get ready, we may be in for a good night yet, so move it.'

After some thought he added 'But she is a redhead, and after Sara I am not sure that I need another redhead. If that Kath has a temper like hers, no, you can leave me out of it. Five months I went out with her, she had a cracking figure and looks but if I looked at her the wrong way, sparks could fly. No thank you, once was enough.'

'Just because she has red hair, it does not say she has a temper like Sara. You have to meet her tonight, you asked Jean if she had a friend for you, we can just go for a drink with them this once.'

'OK just this once.'

Dave finished off his drink and got up, giving Paul a friendly push. 'OK let's go.'

With that they went towards the door leading out of the dining room. As they passed the door into the kitchen, it opened and Kath came out. She looked at Paul giving him a wink and a wave and they both waved back, Paul adding an answering wink.

In the passage outside the dining room, Dave gave Paul a dig in his ribs saying 'Did I say was she saucy or not? Boy, I think you will have your hands full with that one.'

'That is what I am afraid of.'

With that Dave ran to the stairs taking two steps at a time, then he was out of sight around the bend of the stairs leaving Paul who was quite happy taking his time. By the time Paul got to their room Dave was already in the bathroom singing his head off.

Paul smiled as he sat on the bed shouting to Dave, 'Boy, oh boy, have you been struck or what?'

With a lot of ragging they were all spruced up and ready to go.

'OK. Let's go and gave the girls a treat, Paul.'

On entering the bar they noticed the girls were already sitting in the corner. As they made their way over to them they both gave them a wave.

'Well I see you are here before us.'

Paul smiled and sat down beside Kath, Dave stood beside his chair.

'What would you all like to drink?'

Kath asked for a gin and tonic, Jean nodded agreement.

'Lager for you Paul?'

He nodded, not taking his eyes off Kath.

'OK. I'll get them and be here when I get back,' grinned

Dave. A few minutes later he was back with the drinks.

'There you are ladies.'

Passing them their drinks, Dave sat down next to Jean. 'This is what I call cosy, lovely company and a good drink.'

Lifting his glass and looking at Jean Dave added, 'Here's to you ladies, and a pleasurable evening to all.'

They lifted their glasses saying, 'Cheers!'

Looking at Paul, Kath asked if they were on holiday.

'It was Dave's birthday so we decided on a walk over the dales to get some good country air, so here we are with two lovely ladies for company.'

With that Jean turned, put her hands to Dave's shoulders and turning him to her she gave him a full kiss on his lips saying, 'A birthday kiss from me to you.'

Not to be outdone Kath did the same. 'This is from me.'

Paul laughed. 'Girls, you are making him blush. How about me? After all I bought him here.'

Both girls looked at him, leaned over and gave him a peck on the cheek.

'Is that all I get?'

Kath smiled at him. 'Yes, that's all for now but who knows what the night will bring?' Laughing, she patted his cheek.

'I will go and get in a round of drinks while you decide what we are going to do later,' he replied.

While Paul was at the bar Kath asked, 'Has Paul got a girlfriend or wife back home?'

Dave laughed. 'Oh no, not him; though many a girl's tried to hook him, he is still footloose and fancy-free as they say and so am I before you ask. What about you two, anyone special in your lives?'

Looking at Kath, Jean said, 'No we are both as free as birds.'

Then Paul was back carrying the tray on one hand like a waiter and waving with the other. As he sat down Kath said, 'I see you are used to waiting on tables.'

With a wink at Jean as he sat down, he laughed. 'I suppose

I deserved that for showing off.'

They all laughed as they raised their glasses saying 'Down the hatch.'

Jean, smiling at Dave, said, 'Let's stay here for a while and go for a walk in the park later, it's a lovely night and too warm for dancing or pictures. What do you say?'

'I'll drink to that,' said Paul and Dave and together.

After a lot of happy small talk Dave said, 'Did you girls know that the black man was the first man on this planet?'

Jean looked at Dave with surprise. 'What made you say a thing like that? Besides we all know that we were civilised long before them, they were the slaves once; so they could not have been the first men on earth, that's silly.'

They were still having fun arguing about it when Paul put his hand up.

'We have been discussing the subject for over an hour now it's getting late, so let's have one more round, if we are going for a walk we had better go soon. What time do you girls have to be home?'

Kath looked at her watch. 'Let's not have any more to drink, I've had enough.'

Emptying their glasses they all agreed and made their way out. Putting her arm through Paul's, Kath walked him in front of the others; giving Jean the chance to place her arm through Dave's. Minutes later they were in the park walking under a warm clear moonlight sky.

As they got to a fork in the path, Paul turned his head calling to Dave, 'We are taking the right path you can take the left, we will meet you by the gate in an hour. Is that OK with you girls?'

Not waiting for an answer he led Kath to the right. Turning her head she called back 'See you later Jean.'

They had been walking for about five minutes when Kath said, 'Come along, I know a nice quiet spot were we can sit and talk Paul.' Leading him now by his hand, they turned off the path into a small wooded area, until they came to a clearing beside a lake.

'What a lovely surprise, I didn't expect a lake here. Where is this cosy spot you mention?'

Holding him by the shoulder she turned him around. 'There in that recess in the trees, come on.' Kath left him and ran to where she had pointed, throwing herself down on the grass facing the lake.

'Come and join me and see the view.'

'Alright here I come, make room for me.'

Running up to her he threw himself down beside her. 'You were right; it's a lovely quiet place, with a nice view'.

They sat there enjoying the moonlight and watching the ripples playing on the lake, making small talk of it. Paul turned.

'Where is that kiss you promised me back at the hotel, or don't I get one now?'

'I always keep my word, come here let me show you.'

With that she put her arms around his neck, with her lips slightly parted; she kissed him long and hard. As they parted Paul gasped, 'Wow, that was some kiss. Is there any more where that came from?'

Looking at him she laid back putting her hands behind her head, giving him a big smile. 'Why don't you come down here and see?'

Paul leaned over her and putting his hands around her shoulders, gently parted her lips with his, then kissed her, his tongue darting between her lips. In a little while his right hand was fondling her breasts. Undoing her blouse he cupped her nearest breast, then moving from her lips to her exposed nipple, he gently kissed it, caressing it with his tongue. Moving from her breast, he slid his hand down her body, giving gentle squeezes as his hand moved down to her bare legs. His eyes now started to follow the movement of his hand as it gently moved her skirt up to her thighs, exposing her lily-white legs to the moonlight. As his hand reached the hidden mount she gasped, flinging her arms around his head, pulling his lips to hers she savagely kissed him.

Meanwhile Dave and Jean had found their own quiet spot, and laying side by side were indulging themselves in some heavy necking. Dave was exploring her lovely round breasts, gently kissing her hard nipples. Getting excited himself, he let his hand slide down her body, but as he reached her thighs, she caught hold of his hand saying, 'No, this is as far as we can go tonight.'

With that she moved her hand to his zip, sliding it down to the bottom, then moving her hand into his boxer shorts, gasped out, 'Oh my!'

She laughed kissing him with open lips.

Later walking up to the park gates they saw Paul and Kath, both leaning against the gatepost in a tight embrace.

Patting Paul on his shoulder, Dave said, 'Come on, it is time the girls were home.'

Walking on with Dave's arm around Jean's waist, they came to her house. Standing by the gate, Dave asked her what time she would be leaving work tomorrow.

She whispered, 'I will be finished the same time as tonight, so we can meet again in the same place if you like.'

'If I like? Just let anyone try to stop me.'

He smiled as he caught her face in both of his hands, giving her a gentle yet firm kiss.

'Well it's goodnight until tomorrow, sweet dreams, lovely Jean.'

With a laugh she ran up the garden path. She reached the door, and turning blew him a kiss, which he returned. He walked quickly up the road to catch Paul.

Reaching him he put his hand on his shoulder and said, 'You look like the cat that got the cream, I take it that all went well with you and Kath. Will you be seeing her tomorrow, because I have arranged to see Jean.'

'I've never met a girl like her. Fancy having to come all the way out here in the sticks to find the girl I've been looking for. She is nothing like Sara. OK, so you told me, but I had no intentions of going out with another redhead, not after Sara. I've got to see a lot more of her so that I can get my head around this. Anyway, how did you get on with Jean, you seem happy with yourself.'

'Yes, we got on like a house on fire, but like you but I need to get my head sorted out too.'

Walking back to the hotel they were both quiet, hardly a word was said. In their room they both took a shower with only some light banter, until they got into their beds saying their goodnights. Paul lay back with his hands behind his head with a thoughtful smile on his face, while Dave lay with his hands grasped together on top of the bedclothes, smiling contentedly.

The following morning Dave was startled awake by the sound of singing.

'Oh what a beautiful morning, oh what a beautiful day. Come on Dave the sun is shining, the birds are singing, get your lazy self up.'

Dave sat up in bed and picking up his pillow threw it at Paul.

'Shut up, you and your birds, what time is it anyway, it feels like the middle of the night?' Looking at his watch he added, 'Oh lord it's only seven o'clock and I'm on holiday.'

With that he laid back down, pulling the bedclothes over his head. Paul dashed across the room and grabbing the side of the bed, lifted it up tipping Dave onto the floor, then ran into the bathroom singing 'Oh, what a wonderful day' all over again.

Dave sitting up on the floor shouted, 'I'll get you tomorrow, and it will be five o'clock you clown.'

Getting up he remade his bed muttering to himself how he was going to get his own back. He smiled to himself remembering last night, then he too started to sing at the top of his voice, 'Oh what a beautiful morning, oh what a beautiful day.'

Going to the bathroom door Dave shouted, 'Hurry up in there, it's my turn, you've been in there long enough. Come on gave someone else a chance.'

After they had both had their showers and got dressed along with some good-hearted banter, they went down to the dining room for breakfast. Entering the room they looked around, the girls were not there, and as they sat down a young man came over for their order. Giving it to him Paul asked him what time Kath started work. '11 o'clock.' he replied as he walked away to get their order.

Having eaten a leisurely breakfast, they decided to go back to their room to have another look at the capsule.

CHAPTER 3

Bad News

Back in their room, Paul said, 'Dave, let's put the table near my bed, then we can sit or lay back and watch it in comfort.'

'Yes, sounds OK to me.'

Moving the table near to the bed they lifted up the time capsule, putting it in the centre of the table and sat down on the bed.

'I hope it will open again, Paul.'

As Dave stroked his hand along it as before, it opened and the figure of Joseph reappeared.

'You had closed the recorder, if you wish to continue from where we left off, press the yellow button twice.'

Looking down at the buttons Paul pressed the necessary one.

'Dave can you get a pen and paper handy in case we want to write some notes?'

As he said this the figure of Joseph was saying, 'Our world as we had known it, was no more, our beautiful cities and fertile lands were now just barren wastes of sand, all around us was just a sea of it. We wondered if the rest of the planet was like this. Much to our relief we later discovered, most of the land was as it had been and provided that the Ords did not come back to finish what they had started we knew we could survive. Our hope was that the Ords would think the worst. It was seriously worse, as we learned later. 60 per cent of our population worldwide had been destroyed, though not as bad as Mars as we discovered later. Mars was completely wiped out.

'We had not been prepared for anything so devastating, so final. One other matter had us all worried. What had happened to our small moon, which had been in a tighter obit than the present one? When we discovered it was missing, we contacted as many of the survivors as was possible to look, although at the time there did not appear to any adverse affects, it caused some concern.

'Then news started to come in from around the world from other surviving groups, telling us of great tidal waves, of vast floods covering all low-lying lands, washing away towns and villages that had not been decimated by the Ords. Now it was time for us to worry, our land was for the most part low-lying, so it was decided to move to higher ground with as much goods and equipment as possible. Why we were not already under water we did wonder about, thankful whatever the reason; it gave us a chance. Every available platform and flyer was used to shuttle people and goods to the mountains. It was three days before a huge wall of water swept across the plains, until even the pyramids were covered and remained covered for months until the waters receded. We lost a lot of equipment that had been left in the deep underground rooms below the pyramids. The orchards, along with most of our cattle were gone, the underground factories flooded, the specialised robots that ran the factories lost. We were full of dismay at the discovery, many just stood and cried as it began to sink into their minds, no food or clothing factories. Men were sent out on platforms to survey the damage, to gather anything that would be of use to us now and in the future. Some did come back with the good news, there were some untouched orchards in some distant valley, also cattle. This news helped to remove some of the dismay.

'Hundreds of years ago the first world governing body, which was made up equally from all the nations, had banned the making of any weapons or ownership. This had worked very successfully with no more violent crime, between individuals or between nations. It took time but it had worked. Now, looking back with hindsight, did they do the right thing? Could we have avoided all that has happened if we had weapons, taken heed for our future? But then we remembered Mars, they had weapons and it did not help them.

'Now is the time to tell you more about the Ords, how and why they managed to control our worlds, our people. Firstly we never had reason to believe they were an evil race, rather the opposite, they had never used force before on any of the worlds to our knowledge. They had come to us in friendship using their amazing telepathic powers, they gave us pictures in our minds of beautiful cities, a land of plenty, showing us how we could do the same for our world. After a time this was achieved, there was no longer cause to envy friends or neighbours as having more than oneself. We had all we needed or wanted, to work on what made us happy or not work as we chose, we had developed robots to do all the tasks we did not want to do. Yet man being man, there were those among us not happy about it. We realised that we were losing our own incentive to think and develop. We were in a rut, life was getting too easy, all play and no work unless we wanted to. It was not man's way. We were our own makers of our lives, to do and invent. We began to form discussion groups which got bigger and bigger, we visited other planets and began to become well organised. We were quite open about it, we did not think that the Ords would react against us, but they did by trying to influence our minds. It did work on many of us, but by now most of us were able to close our minds to the Ords. It was not just us, but the Chinese and the Red Indians too were feeling as we did; it had been foolish of us not to consider how the Ords would react. Although the Ords could use and did use their telepathic powers to suppress, or guide man away from discontent, there were an increasing number of us who could close their minds to the them. We are the descendants of those, the malcontents who wanted more, more of what, who can say now after all this time? Probably freedom of thought, the freedom to do things ourselves without being guided by others.

'It was gradually becoming apparent that many could close their minds to the Ords. They could no longer repress our minds, we knew that something was missing from our lives. Once this knowledge was recognised by many of our peoples, including the Chinese and the Red Indians, we found the same was happening on their worlds, more and more of them could repress the Ords' power over them.

'Over time the Ords discovered this discord, and made plans to remove all those who could close their minds to them. They made plans to separate us, they had already discovered this planet and had disposed of most of the large animals that had inhabited it for future colonisation.

'They picked this planet partly because it was small, and compatible with our own worlds. The other reason was that we three races had always been at loggerheads with each other. Before the Ords came we had often made war on each other, always over some misunderstanding, man being what he was, a creature ready to fight with or without reason. The coming of the Ords did stop all that. So they picked this planet we believe, because it had three separate land masses, one for each race.

'There were two groups of Ords. Most of them were small, about three feet tall, with small thin bodies and big heads, large oval black eyes, but no ears as we have and small mouths. The others were twice as tall, with thin bodies but with smaller heads, these were mostly healers or surgeons, they had long delicate fingers.

'They built their robots in the image of themselves, their brains were almost as good as man's, but a lot quicker. They were used for deep space travelling and exploring new worlds; their scout ships could turn at right angles at astounding speeds, which the human body could not stand. The tall robots were good surgeons, but because they could not understand pain, they were not very popular. Both kinds also worked in the factories and on the farms, but they had all been programmed to do various work.'

'Hold it Paul, I need to go to the toilet. Tell you what, how about going down for another drink, I need one.'

'OK, what about this machine, shall we just switch it off and leave it? The maid has already changed the beds, so there is no need to worry about anyone else coming in.'

'You are right, just switch it off and leave it, we won't be all that long.'

Discussing what they had been listening to over a couple of beers, Dave said, 'It takes a lot of swallowing. History will be blown out of the window if this gets out, you don't think it's somebody's idea of a joke do you? Hell, no it can't be, that machine is way beyond anything we can make today, I keep saying this, what are we going to do with it?'

'Look, let's just listen to it, we can worry about what to do with it when it has finished. There may be something we have not heard yet that may decide it for us, let's just wait.'

'You know there is something else that I keep thinking about.'

'Well now what? You worry too much Dave. Anyway out with it, what else is bothering you?'

'That last bit when he was describing what the Ords and what their robots look like. It's strange, but it is the way people have described the aliens from those flying saucers. It struck me when we were listening to their description, I wonder if what they saw were the Ords' robots.

'You are right. Come to think about it, it's uncanny how their description fits. I remember laughing to myself when I saw the pictures in the paper, thinking, how did they come up with a creature like that? If this gets out we won't laugh at them any more.'

Finishing off the drinks they made their way back to their room.

'Dave, let's get a couple of chairs and make ourselves comfortable, then we will see what other surprises it has in store.'

This time it was Paul who moved his hand along the cylinder, it opened as before.

'Go on Dave, I will let you have the honour of switching it on.'

Dave pressed the button to continue from were they had left off, Joseph reappeared as before. Now he was saying, 'Our world as we had known it was no more, our beautiful cities and fertile lands were now barren wastes, parts of the planet had been changed by the floods. In China a lot of the land was under water, there were now many islands, some quite big. The island you call Japan was now separated from the mainland, there were many other parts changed.

'Our biggest concern was the disappearance of Atlantis which was on the continent of the place you called Antarctica. It was our largest city, built by all three races, a city of enjoyment for all, people would go there for relaxation from all over. It was a city like no other, there were old-fashioned sailing ships on the river that flowed though the city. It had been a city of dreams, now there was just water. We did not know it at first, but it was because the axis of the planet had been changed by the bombardment, the destruction of our small moon. Outlines of the city could still be seen, but of the million or more people there was no sign.

'We will now go back to when the Ords brought us here, but to gave you a clearer and more defined picture, we will no longer use the hologram. Stand at the end of this capsule, point the beam of light that will appear at a plain wall.

Dave and Paul moved as directed; they saw a tube with a round ball appear from near the centre of the cylinder, then a beam of light came from the ball right into the corner of the room.

Paul looked at Dave and said, 'That won't do, let's face the beam to that wall at that end of the room,' pointing to the far wall that had a picture of the moors hanging on it.

'Let's take the picture down and move the dresser out of the way as well.'

They lifted the table with the cylinder so that the beam was shining onto the end wall, taking the picture down that was in centre of it, and also moved the dresser out of the way. Now there was just a plain wall and they moved the dresser until the beam of light expanded and it was only a few inches from the top and bottom of the wall.

They were now looking at a picture that was three-dimensional, as though they were looking out of a window. They appeared to be there in the picture, it was uncanny, feeling as if they could reach out and touch Joseph. He started to speak again.

'When the ship bringing us here was in orbit, we were told that we would be landed on the planet by remote control, the guards would be returning to the home world in a scout ship that had come with us. When the ship landed the food stores would be left open for us, the food should last for four months, and from then on we were expected to live off the land. According to history everyone was at this point still locked into their seats, which was just as well or there would have pandemonium. The ship had been divided into two sections which nether the women or the men knew about. Both sexes had been unaware that they were both on the same ship, each thinking that they would be marooned without members of the opposite sex. The ship landed on the land mass you know as Europe, and until this moment they had all been locked in their seats. Shortly after they had landed the locks were released and both sides of the ship opened and everyone scrambled out. The men all came out of one side and the women the other, neither knowing. It was quite some time before they found each other because of the size of the ship and when they did get together there was much shouting and dancing. They were happier still when they realised there were no guards. Couples slowly began to pair off, but not without some fights when one or the other fancied the same person.

'As you can will understand it took months to organise

ourselves, there were too many wanting to be headman. At first they formed committees, then sub-committees to take control of groups of about five hundred couples each, once these were formed the groups were spread out over a larger area, each group was given an equal share of the equipment and stores.

'There were no weapons of any kind to be found on the ship, but they were overjoyed to find hundreds of small robots stored in the nose of the ship, these were the three foot tall units. They also found that each one had a variable programme, which allowed them to perform specialised work such as doctors, chemists, horticulturists and many more. The normal working life of a robot was a hundred years. Knowing this they believed they could rebuild a life similar to that which they had been used to. They also discovered hundreds of anti-gravity platforms, both large and small so they now had means of transport. The general consensus was that the Ords were not so bad after all, they had left them with all they needed to start a new life, be it far from their friends and loved ones which they realised that they were not going to see again. They had decided to build the main and first town here, where they had landed and eight groups were to have this task. The rest of the groups were to spread out to build smaller towns, when they found a suitable place. They were to go out in at least two groups, so that they had the manpower to build their towns. These groups sent out scouts on the small anti-gravity platforms with three men to each. Their task was to find suitable locations for their groups to settle and build. The more adventurous travelled hundreds of miles before deciding on the location they liked. Although they were not to know at this time, there were two other continents which had been settled, in much the same manner as theirs, by other races that the Ords had transported to this planet.

'They worked hard for many years until villages and small towns were built. They were happy, they began to look to the future which was full of promise and as the populations grew they began to extend further afield, building more and more towns. Commerce began to grow between the towns and villages.

'It was at this about time in our history that men began to wonder whether there were other lands on the other side of the seas and the young men became obsessed with the thoughts of discovering new lands. The first adventurers that embarked were only two hundred, mainly because of the large anti-gravity platforms. By now only ten remained in good working order and it was decided to keep these for the heavy work still needed to carry on building the towns. There were only twenty medium ones that could carry twenty-five men in comfort left, although we still had lot of the small five-man ones in good condition. Unfortunately there was no one with the knowledge to make new ones, nor the material or equipment, even the robots had not been implanted with the knowledge. However we did use four of the medium ones, which could carry twenty-five men each. On each one we only sent four men, allowing room to carry anything extra that they might find; these were trips of exploration and salvage.

'It was a hot summer's day when they set off along the four points of the compass, north, south, east and west. The first group back had gone north reporting that they had only discovered a cold waste land mass covered with ice and snow.

'The second to arrive back had gone to the west across a vast sea. They brought the news we had hoped for, that we were not alone on this planet by bringing back visitors, twenty red men who had come from the planet Mayho. They had been brought here like us, which was not really surprising. They were as aggressive in nature as we had been, there had been conflict between us for hundreds of years. Now we had been thrown together on the same planet, what this would mean for our futures? We would have to wait and see. On the journey home to us both parties had got on well, it had been an exciting meeting with everyone treating one another like long-lost brothers. However at this first meeting we were all more excited by the knowledge that we were not alone, than concerned about worrying about our past strife. Days later we had another surprise, when the men who had gone south returned with the news that this planet was already inhabited, by a black race of humans. These were a much younger race than ours and at very primitive stage, more like our ancient ancestors, and because of our colour and the way we had appeared out of the sky, they thought we were gods.

"There were more shocks when the group came back from the east, there they discovered that some Chinese had also been transported here. These were a yellow race who had always been hard to get along with, now they were also on this small planet they began to wonder why. Three aggressive races that had been in conflict for hundreds of years are suddenly put together on a small planet. However at the time there were plenty of other things to worry about, now we knew that there were three races here not counting the local black race. When the excitement had died down, we learnt all about the Mayhos, how they were tackling their problems. They like us had built towns and villages around one main one, spreading out and finding places to settle in small groups. They did get new ideas from them as they did from us. After weeks showing our visitors our towns and villages, the time came for them to return them back to their own people. It had been a very friendly meeting, which was surprising because of the past conflict between our races, which had lasted for hundreds of years. Maybe this was a new beginning for us all? Time would tell. We wondered about the Chinese, how would we get on with them in the future since they had not welcomed our scouting party. Instead they had made it clear that they had no wish to have any contact with us. Maybe time would improve that, at the moment they had plans of their own to fulfil.'

Putting his hand on Dave's shoulder, Paul said, 'I've had

enough for now. Let's go and get a drink, I'm parched.'

Looking a bit dazed, Dave looked at him. 'Bloody hell, this is going to turn our history books upside down alright. I still can't take it all in, and yes, I do need a drink, no, make that two drinks and switch it off for now. Like you, I need a rest from it.'

Getting up and having a good stretch Paul then switched off the machine. He looked at his watch.

'It's nearly one-thirty, they stop serving lunch at two, come on let's move.'

They put the machine away back under the bed, tidied themselves up then dashed off to the dining room.

CHAPTER 4

Second Date

As Dave and Paul entered the dining room Jean was tidying the table they had been on yesterday. She looked up and her face broke into a big smile. She waved them over to the table but they were already halfway to her, still beaming at them.

'You are late, I was worried something had happened.'

'Well now, we can't have a pretty girl like you getting worried can we?'

Brushing up close to her with his lips almost touching hers, Dave sat down as Jean handed him a menu, with a little blush.

'Can I take your order Sir?'

Giving her a wink, he handed over the menu to Paul. 'You order Paul, while I admire the view.'

Jean whispered, 'Stop it, you will get me into trouble.'

She moved over to Paul's side of the table. 'What would you like Sir?'

Paul smiled at her. 'I like the way you say "Sir".'

Dave give Paul a gentle punch on his arm. 'Stop teasing her and order something, or we will be too late to get anything. I will have roast beef, Yorkshire pudding, carrots and cabbage please Miss.'

'OK, Miss I will have the same followed by apple pie with custard.'

'Make that two, please.'

With the same little skip as yesterday, Jean went away with the order. Later as they were drinking a lager each, Jean came back with her tray to clear the table.

'Will we be seeing you tonight?'

Paul was still feeling mischievous. 'No, I think we will sit on that blonde's table for dinner tonight. What do you think Dave?'

Jean took a little step back.

'Don't take any notice of him, if you had heard him raving about Kath earlier. He's just teasing, so think of something nice for us all to do tonight, that is if Kath can come. She will come, won't she?'

Giving him a big smile, Jean replied, 'Of course she will, meet you in the bar at eight o'clock then.'

As she passed Paul, she gave him a little push. 'You.'

Then she was gone; a couple of minutes later they saw Kath blowing them a kiss from the kitchen door.

As they finished their drinks Dave said, 'What about going for a walk before we look at the capsule again, I need a rest from it.'

'Fine, it's a good idea, let's have a look around in daylight.'

Leaving the hotel they decided to retrace the walk they had taken the night before with the girls. They were surprised by how far the park was from the hotel, as Dave remarked when they got to the park gates.

'Don't forget Dave, we had the girls with us last night, and our minds were not thinking about distances, at least mine wasn't. Kath has really got to me like no other girl. She is fun to be with, a damn good looker and I find her easy to talk to. I could get serious with her, good heavens, what am I saying?'

'I think you are falling for her in a big way. What has happened to the guy who has always said, "Love them and leave them"? Mind you I am beginning to feel that way about Jean. Now that would be something, us going home, telling our parents we were serious with a girl we met on our holidays.'

'Dave, if I go home and tell my mother that, she would start arranging the marriage there and then, there would be nothing she would like better. Stop it. Hell, I just mentioned the word, marriage; let's talk about something else.'

'A good point, I say. It's quite a nice park, plenty of flowers and seats.'

Not much was said until they came to the lake, where they decided to sit for a while. Paul laid down with his hands behind his head, turning to Dave.

'I've been thinking, when we get home we will have to make a video copy, that is before we pass the capsule over to the authorities. If we decide to hand it over, I can see it causing a lot of trouble if it becomes general knowledge.'

'Let us wait until we have seen it all before we start worrying. Let's forget about it for now, relax. That was the idea of coming for this walk, and of course to talk about the girls, when you so nicely changed the subject.'

'Yes, changing the subject, OK, I have to do some serious thinking about Kath, she is really getting to me, and damn it, I like it.'

'We have only just met them, they may be just having fun with us. Let's wait, our holiday's just started.'

'Yes, Dave you are right, let's just lie here and enjoy the peace and quiet.'

After spending over an hour lazing in the park and wandering around the few shops, they went back to the hotel bar, where they spent some more time over a couple of drinks, before going back to their room and setting up the capsule.

CHAPTER 5

The Aftermath

Back in their room Dave and Paul reset the machine and made themselves comfortable.

Joseph began, 'After we had got over the surprises, and the news that our scouts had brought us, we carried on with our building and commerce. As the populations grew, new towns were built further afield, then the inevitable happened. More of the anti-gravity sleighs began to lose their power; there was little we could do about them, since as I have already said, we did not have the means to replace the power. The robots were not programmed to rebuild, or to repair themselves without electricity. This was a big blow to us as more and more failed. However while the robots were still functional, the heavy work of building and suchlike could still be done. The robots lasted sixty years after the anti-gravity sleds broke down, and it came as a big blow, for although we knew the day would come, we had still not prepared ourselves for it happening.

'The towns where they broke down first wanted the towns who had some still working to give them some of theirs, and when they refused they were stolen. As a result fights broke out between towns. They began to fortify their towns with ramparts, crude weapons were made and commerce broke down. Another thing that upset people was that there were no factories making clothes. With no replacements available, they were now wearing rags instead of the beautiful clothes they had been used to; people were being robbed just for their clothes. Now they also had to look after the fields to grow their own food and no one had any knowledge of how to grow crops or what and when to grow. This had all been left to the robots for hundreds of years, and those that managed to grow something had to fight to keep it. The world was slowly returning to barbarism. People began to move out of the towns in groups and became scavengers of the countryside, stealing from other groups and villagers. Some settled in caves and passage shelters that had been made before the holocaust. Those that still had corpses in them were cleared out, the remains taken and dumped away from their sites. People were now spreading throughout Europe, first in small groups, and these in turn joined up with others because now it was safer.

'We who had remained in and around the pyamids were now getting old. At the making of this chronicle, I myself had reached the age of 194 years and later on in this chronicle one of my grandsons will be taking over; hopefully we will still be able to record events that are happening for a long time yet. Because we are in the middle of a desert, which had been a beautiful fertile land, we have been left alone for a long time by the peoples of Europe. We were able to use our anti-gravity platforms including our bubble transports, which were fast and not so easy to see in the air, so we have been able to see how the world as we once knew it was collapsing. We have tried to influence some of the groups with material and information. It worked for a short time until they started to rely on us too much, it was decided to leave them to discover for themselves.

'It was at this time when our scientists had time on their hands for other studies that they noticed that the moon appeared to appear in the sky at a different position, but of our small moon there was still no sign. We assumed that it had been thrown out of orbit, possibly out towards the stars or our own sun; if it had just been destroyed there should have some sign of it. On checking the position of the sun, it also appeared to be on a different angle. We checked it again a day later, and the earth appeared to be still changing its angle of axis. It was only minimal but it was giving us grave concern so it was decided to keep recording any movement that took place. What we needed was a permanent computer to record data for many years to come; we would need to know if and when the earth returned to its original axis, and the instruments that could have made this easy had been destroyed in the great flood.

'With many months of debate it was decided to set out a simple form of computer, using large stones. Later in a clear area of land in northern Europe, we built our first one, this work was done using robots and anti-gravity platforms, but when it was completed it was found that the stones were not tall enough to commute all that information we needed. While we were discussing how to overcome this problem, it was brought to our attention that in the western hills of the large island of Dormas, the one you call Britain, large blue stones were found in the part you call Wales across the water from us, and there was plenty of stone that could be cut as large as we needed.'

Dave gripped Paul's arm saying excitedly, 'That island is Britain, there appears to be more of it; look along the East Coast from where Bridlington is today. Look we are moving inland now.

'Wow, there is Stonehenge, look at its size. There must be hundreds more stones than there are today, there are long lines of them as well as more larger circles. When we went to see it a couple of years ago, it looked like a small huddle of stones, in your words. I know now why it disappointed us, this is what we were expecting to see.'

'Yes I thought that too, shut up and let's pay attention to what he's saying.'

Now they were looking at a quarry with hundreds of robots, lifting stones that would need a couple of cranes today.

'Look at that, he is showing us how they cut the stones. Well I'm damned, look at those robots on that quarry face, can you see that one there pointing with his index finger? It's got a light coming from it, I bet that is a laser beam. They must be measuring it by eye, they are not using a tape or anything. I wonder why they are cutting from the bottom upwards, look at that other robot, it is sliding a platform under it, I bet it is the anti-gravity platform.'

They were floating behind, and to one side of the robots working on the stone they were watching. Paul had a serious expression on his face.

'I hope we stay in this position until they finish cutting that stone. I want to see how they move it because that laser beam is very narrow, it is going to be a tight fit and will have to drop down very straight to get it out.'

'That fooled you Paul, they are pulling it straight out not dropping it down.'

'I never did believe the historians saying that the stones were cut with some sort of hand chisel, it would have been impossible to get them dead square as they did. This is most certainly going to cause a lot of debate if, or when it gets out,' Paul said, looking at Dave.

'Debate, don't you mean a revolution, all those scholars and archaeologists who have written books explaining their theories. If we let this out we had better be a long way away, and out of sight, or they will have our guts for garters.

'I know what you mean, it will be bad enough finding out that the black man may have been the original inhabitant of this world.'

'I wonder if they built Stonehenge – or is it Avesbury – first.'

'Look at those platforms, they must be floating about six foot off the ground and look at the size of that block of stone. That robot is guiding it with just one hand, or is he pushing it?'

'There appears to be a fan on the back of the platforms, can you see them Paul? It looks as if the robots are just guiding them, I was wondering how they got them across the rivers, but I reckon the robots would have ridden them across as well.'

Paul said, pointing, 'Do you notice how thick that platform is, it must be a good eight to ten inches, that is where the anti-gravity device must be. I wish we could see it in more detail.'

'You can, if we can find one of the canisters he spoke of earlier, the ones with the technical information. Gosh, wouldn't that be something finding one of those? I hope they gave us a clue in this one of where to find them. What a difference it would make, space travel for starters.'

'Look who's talking now.'

Now they were back at Stonehenge. There were men and women instructing the robots, it appeared as though they were showing them where to place the stones. They could see robots holding L-shaped poles, other robots were placing the stones into the holes and when they were in line with the poles, others filled them.

'Look Dave how easy it was putting the cross stones up. They just put stones on a small anti-gravity platform, and up it goes, easy when you know how.'

'We must be looking at Stonehenge much later, because we are now looking at small groups of men and women, walking among the stones, all talking into something much like a hand calculator. They are recording the movement of the sun rays hitting different stones. Dave, I believe this is to do with them thinking the earth's orbit has changed, they will have to check it often for at least a year, probably a lot longer to check with the stars as well.'

'I think you are right Paul, it stands to reason after what we have seen and heard.'

Joseph again began to speak. 'We built many stone computers around the planet, we needed to know if the orbit had stopped changing. If it had not we would be in for a rough time. As it was, it stayed at 7 degrees off its original axis.'

The scene changed. Now they were looking down from high above, seeing a long line of the platforms, some with men sitting on them, others with small robots and each one holding a small box and moving their fingers across them.

Dave leaned forward. 'Look the men are light brown – or are they sun-tanned – yes, I think so, they must be white and tanned. They look like Romans with those short tunics, except for those with coloured pantaloons on. There must be hundreds of tonnes of stone on that lot. Look they are coming up to a river, I wonder how they are going to cross it? Hell of course, if they can float over land they can float over water.'

The scene changed again.

'You are right, they are moving just the same as if there was no river. By the way, you do realise we are back over Egypt, Dave?'

'Yes Paul. What we could do with those platforms. No need for roads or bridges, just float up and down, down and up, no problem. There is a small platform with a bubble over it, look at that woman with those two men. Gosh, she is beautiful, hope we get a closer look at her. Damn we are going away from them.' Then they were moving very fast in the same direction as the platforms were heading.

'Look, we are heading back to the city.'

As they neared it they saw that there was another line of platforms, with blocks of stone on them, also another long line of empty ones coming away from the city, running parallel with the in-going line. Then they were over a park that extended to the other end of the city, it looked about half a mile wide from where they were. Now they were hovering above the base of a pyramid, there were robots carrying the blocks of stone as if they were just large empty cardboard boxes, fitting them one on top of the other in perfect position.

'Look, they are placing the blocks around a big square hole; it is deep too. Dave, can you imagine how long it would take us today, just to put one block in the correct position? They could position a dozen to our one, we always thought that it would have taken them years, I suppose it would have if they had to do it with manpower alone, which I never really believed.'

Joseph was saying, 'Did you notice the tall structures on the hills as we approached the city, those are the negative ionisers which we have installed all over the planet. Over many years our scientists discovered there were waves of positive ions moving slowly around the planet, and where they lingered they appeared to fetch out the worst in people, resulting in more violence, even wars. It was then that they started to experiment with negative ions. First they made small machines, these they installed in assembly halls where there were always heated arguments, and tempers were short. These experiments proved to be very successful, tempers and arguments became less. Next people had them in their homes with reports that the air appeared fresher to breathe, the atmosphere in the homes became more relaxed, people were happier. There was another surprising benefit; when the negative ion box was placed on an arm, or other part of the body that had a pulled muscle, or a pain, after a few minutes it would go away. It was then that they were made smaller and shaped to other body parts, every household had them. They are also in the medical cubicles scattered around all our cities. These cubicles are there for anyone to have an instant medical check up, blood pressures and samples and such like can be dealt with there and then.

'It took many years before the idea of placing large ionisers around the world was accepted, once this was completed the world settled down to peace and harmony. Maybe this had something to do with the Ords' war on us, we don't know and may never know now. By now you will have an idea of our history, hopefully you will not have made the same mistakes that we have.'

'Come, Dave let's go for a drink. I think we should discuss everything with a drink in each hand.'

They both laughed as Paul switched the capsule off, and grabbing their jackets they made their way to the bar.

'I don't know why we are laughing, we have a problem. This is real serious stuff. What are we going to do with it? The more I see of it the more I worry.'

'Stop worrying. I told you before, let's wait until we get home, so come on it's your round.'

'Worrying, what have you two got to worry about?'

They both turned around on their stools and there was Jean standing beside them with an empty tray in her hand.

Dave put his hand on Jean's arm saying, 'Now then my lovely, me worried? Now what have I to be worried about with a beautiful girl like you going out with me?'

'I heard Paul say for you to stop worrying. Sorry but I had only stopped to say hello, I wasn't listening to you.'

'Don't worry your little head over it, we were just discussing something we had come across. Come on, give me a kiss.'

'Stop it you will get me sacked! Anyway what are we doing tonight, have you anything nice planned?'

'That, my young lady, is one of the things we were talking about, now off you go and we will see you later.'

CHAPTER 6

Committed

'Well girls, here we are all ready and willing, now what about a few drinks before we go out? Same as yesterday or do you want a change?'

'I think we will have our usual. Alright with you Kath?'

Kath nodded.

'Yes, shall we find a table, our usual one is empty.'

Carrying their drinks they went to the table and sat down all looking happy with smiles all round.

'Here's to you girls, let's drink to a pleasant night for all.'

'Come on Dave it includes you, lift up your glass.'

Clinking glasses together they all laughed

'Dave, now what is bothering you? You look as if you have the worries of the world on your shoulders. Come on, snap out of it.'

'Oh, there is nothing bothering me, I have just been thinking.'

'Well share it with us. We may be able to help you.'

'Maybe tomorrow, let me think about it.'

'I am OK now, let me get us some more drinks, same again everyone?'

They all nodded as Dave got up, laughed and kissed Jean on the cheek.

A few minutes he was back with the drinks.

'There you are all served with a smile, everyone happy now? I was going to get us all doubles but as it is still early, one at a time would be best.'

Looking up at him and patting him on both cheeks, Jean said, 'That's my boy, come closer I want to kiss you, lover.'

'Now look what you've done, you've made him blush,'

remarked Paul giving Dave a friendly push.

'You leave him alone you bully, I think it's sweet.' So saying Jean put her arm through Dave's, pulling him closer to her and giving him a big smile.

Dave picked up his drink, 'Bottoms up everyone, let's decide what or where are we going tonight.'

'Let's do something I have been thinking about for a while. Let's go to our room and show them our time capsule, I would like to find out how they will react. It may help us to decide what we will do about it later.'

Looking startled Dave put his hand on his arm. 'I don't think that is such a good idea, we should think a bit more about it. Anyway you should have discussed it with me first.'

Kath looked into Paul's face.

'Now what are you up to? A time capsule indeed, is this a ruse to get us into your bedroom? What will they come up with next?'

'It is a new one on me.' Both girls laughed.

'No, it is something we found when were coming across the moors. I just want your reaction to it, maybe as Dave says, we can think about it.'

'Oh no you don't, you can't get us intrigued then try to put us off. We are not going to let you get away with it, are we Jean?'

'No, come on, what is it all about? We are coming to your room now whether we are invited or not. Come on drink up, I want to see what you have, and you had better have this capsule, or whatever.'

'Now see what you've done Paul. We have no choice now so let's get it over with.' So saying Dave downed his drink telling the others to do the same.

They all finished off their drinks and marched out of the bar, Dave leading the way but not looking very happy.

Dave was still in the lead when they got to the door, turning to them. 'Are you sure about this Paul?'

'Go on, open it.'

Dave opened the door letting the girls in first. Paul followed, going straight to the bed.

'Come on girls, you sit on the bed while Dave and I set it up.'

'Do you think it's safe Jean? I mean here we are in their bedroom, sitting on their bed.'

'Be quiet Kath, I am sure they have something to show us.'

'I know, but what?' she said with a mischievous smile on her face.

At that moment Paul and Dave pulled the cylinder from under the bed.

Putting it on the table Paul said, 'OK, get it going Dave, we can carry on from where it left off. Girls, what you are going to see is going to surprise you. This is a time capsule and what you are going to see, and hear, is our world as it was thousands of years ago. We have been watching it every day since we came here, so you are going to watch it from where we left off. We can all see it from the beginning later, that is, if you want to.'

Both girls were looking at the capsule in surprise.

'You were serious, you do have a capsule. What does it do?' gasped Kath.

'Well if you both pull up a chair each, and sit behind the table we will show you.'

'Alright Dave open up and switch on.'

As Dave ran his hand over the capsule it opened, and both girls gave a gasp moving back.

'It is OK, just look at the wall.'

Dave pressed the button and Joseph appeared. Again there was a look of surprise from both girls as he started to speak.

'Now I would like you to see the rest of the planet before and after the destruction of it. First we will go to the land of the Mayas, South America as you have called it.'

Then they were over the sea, heading to land that was clearly seen on the horizon. At first they were flying over vast lush forests, and low enough to see what appeared to be monkeys, then they had a surprise as they flew over large plantations of palm trees.

Here, Joseph was talking again. 'These were the coconut farms. As you can see it is run by robots and black men. For this service we feed and clothe them, give them good houses to live in and they get along with the robots just fine.'

There appeared to be miles of trees, all in neat rows as if they had been measured out.

'It is from these that we get our oils and of course foods, it is not possible for me to explain the finer points of their use. Although there will be some men and women who could give you more information, it is not my field of expertise, it is left mainly to the robots.

'We are now heading northwards, here you will see how well we have organised everything. As you will know this is the land of the Mayas, but each continent produces food, equipment or whatever it is best suited for, to provide for the rest of the planet. Some make the robots that work the farms, others produce the robots that build others, most of the factories are underground and away from the cities. This way the beauty of the countryside is left unmarked.

'All the produce is sent to every part of the planet wherever it is required. We have no monetary system, we have no need now that there is enough of everything for all. Computers control what is needed and where; for the most part goods are sent by underground except where it is necessary to go overseas, then it is transported by air on large anti-gravity platforms. They are more like large floating squares, usually about twenty-five of your feet wide. Sometimes these ships will pick up and drop off their cargoes from factory to factory, although they can fly at any height they do not travel over towns or cities.

'We are now passing over the fruit plantations, as you can see below us are the orange groves.'

'How beautiful it all looks, those must be lemons, over there those look like grapefruit.'

Jean was leaning forward for a better look, turning to Dave with a look of excitement on her face.

'Oh, Dave it's just wonderful. What a world to live in, was it really like this, miles and miles of fruit all in neat lines? I wish we could walk along them.'

Looking at her, Dave said, 'Don't get too carried away with it, all that is well gone now.'

'But it could be again.'

'Yes, maybe sometime in the future, who knows? It could be, if man will learn to live without wars, without wanting what the other man has, to live in harmony with each other in a true sense.'

They were now moving again, very fast, and the countryside they were passing over was just a blur. As they were coming into sight of another city, everything slowed down. This city was built in circles, in the centre was one large structure and moving out from it were roundly built houses. These were all in a green shade of colour, very beautiful, as both the girls said together. Some of the houses were on straight or spiral columns, they were all circled at the first floor by a wide platform. As they were watching there were flying machines, or more aptly flying bubbles, landing on them and people were either getting on or off them. It was the largest city they had seen so far, stretching for what appeared to be miles, and in the distance they could see floating houses at all different heights.

Joseph was talking again. 'If you look to the top right-hand side you will see a partly built pyramid; because they have no parks within the city itself, they are making theirs on the outskirts of their cities.'

Paul said, 'Look girls, can you see that square building with all those robots milling around? It is only half finished but you can see that it is going to be a pyramid.'

They were now almost over it. Now they could see the robots with the platforms, some with large stones, but not the big blocks that they had seen in Egypt. These were just stones but they would be too heavy for them to lift. Joseph interrupted their concentration by interjecting, 'As you will see they have no large blocks of stone with which to build them, but they will be using a special cement that they have made, that hold the pyramids together. This will help it to withstand the heaviest of blasts, we can only hope and wait.'

The girls were enthralled with what they were seeing, each one pointing in turn to something that caught their eye. They were flying very high up so they had a bird's eye view of most of the city. There must have been hundreds of flying machines in the air, which appeared to have no controlled lanes or levels to be flying in, yet although some appeared to be heading into another, none of them did crash. There must be some sort of control but they could not see how.

Now they were over a city that appeared so big they could not see the far outskirts.

Suddenly Paul caught hold of Dave's arm. 'Look, I never noticed it before, the people are standing still, but they are still moving, look they have moving pavements. There appears to be a solid pavement, and moving ones either side of it. Now that is what I call a good idea.'

'No, I didn't see before, I wonder how many other things we have missed. Still we will see it all over again.'

Joseph was saying, 'Below us is the Mayas' largest city called Quetos, in the part you called Brazil, as you can see they have many parks like us, they also enjoy a carefree life. Although they have not built their pyramids yet, they will be built in their parks as we have over the whole planet.'

The city below them was not as gracious as some they had seen, but the parks were the biggest with orange and other fruit groves, trees and flowers which made it all a scene beyond description. The girls were entranced, grasping each other's hands, putting their hands to their faces with gasps of delight. Dave and Paul were all smiles as they watched the girls.

Now they were moving again, still flying high and getting an overall picture of the land. They noticed that most of the populated areas were along the coast in South America, which they were now passing over.

'Look Dave, that must be the Gulf of Mexico down there. Have you noticed how green the land and everything is? I know most of it is trees except for the mountains and plateaus, wish we could have a closer look.'

'I agree with you Paul. I wonder what sort of animals are in those jungles? I suppose it would depend on how far back it is in time. I haven't seen anything that gives a clue, have you?'

'No, I guess not, we must keep a close look at everything, there must be something to give us a clue.'

'Notice the girls are in a world of their own, they have hardly said a word to us for ages.'

Kath looked at him and laughed. 'It is so interesting and exciting. You should have shown us this before. Anyway quiet, I don't want to miss anything.'

Dave looked at Paul giving him a shrug of his shoulders.

Joseph was saying, 'If you look we are now over the biggest freight terminal. This continent supplies most of the goods and produce for the rest of the planet, also most of the robots and platforms for the central continent.'

Below them they could see a vast area of level ground covered in large images of animals and birds, and running off into the distance were parallel lines.

'The markings you see represent the parts of the planet that the goods are going to, the robots who control, and those that load the transport ships know where to load from.'

They could see large long flat platforms being loaded by the smaller ones, like the ones they had seen earlier in the fields loaded with produce. They were being loaded in rows of three abreast and eight long. One of them to their right appeared to be fully loaded, the team of robots who had been loading it all got onto a small platform. This flew away from the large one which then appeared to be covered in a transparent film.

As they were wondering what it was, Joseph said, 'You may notice that there is now an energy field surrounding one of the ships which is ready to take off, this is to keep the cargo dry on its crossing of the sea. We are now coming up to the most populated area in North America. This is where most of the factories are that make the robots, the flying machines and where a great deal of our foods are produced. You will see a lot more of the factories above ground here mainly because there is the space for them. As you will also see, they are well away from the populated areas. We are now flying across your country of America. As you will notice there are different areas for different crops, there are the grain growing fields and others with all our various fruits.'

They were passing over vast areas of land which appeared to grow just about anything they could think of, all set out in neat rows. They could see robots everywhere, with a variety of machines going up and down the rows collecting the crops. In the centre of each growing area there were large buildings, to which the robots were taking the produce they had collected. At the end of the factories were large platforms which, once loaded, lifted up to what looked to be about a hundred feet off the ground, and then flew off in different directions.

They passed a number of houses, most of them on the ground, sometimes just a few together, others in small groups or towns. There were also some scattered along some mountains, usually in twos or threes high up near the peaks. There were no large cities as they had seen elsewhere in South America, there were as many houses but scattered in small groups.

Joseph was speaking again. 'We will be approaching some islands shortly, I would like you to see what lengths we went to, deceiving the Ords when building the pyramids. Here we are. Many came to the island below us to build statues, you can see them being made.'

They were looking down onto a man and woman, directing a robot who was shaping the end of a large block of stone, rounding off about four to five feet. As they watched it the robot started to cut a circle on the ground, using a laser beam from its forefinger. After what seemed like only a few minutes, it got a long rod which appeared to be made of glass, and held it in the centre of the circle it had made. A pale blue light came from the end of it, then it sank into the ground until about two feet of it remained. The robot slowly turned it, lifted it out and put it to one side. Another robot came over and between them they lifted a round plug of earth and rock straight up from the ground, took it over to the cliff and threw it into the sea. Walking over to the block of stone that had been rounded off, the two of them picked it up, carried it to the hole they had made and dropped it into it as a perfect fit.

The man then started to shape it with a hand-held laser, looking along the row of other statues. They all looked different, all of them hideous monstrosities.

'Dave, can you remember what that island is called?'

'No, and at the moment I don't care, I need a drink.'

Dave switched off the capsule. 'That's it everyone, I am ready for a drink, what about it?'

The girls looked up at the boys. 'OK.'

Jean stood up. 'We will go for a drink, I'm ready for one, but we want to come back to see more. It's weird when you think about it, an advanced civilisation all those thousands of years ago. Anyway I need a drink so let's go. What time is it someone? Don't forget the bar closes at eleven o'clock.'

Looking at his watch as he helped Paul to put the machine away, Dave said, 'It is just gone ten so we will have time for a couple if we get a move on.'

With that they all rushed down to the bar, Paul and Dave

ordering the drinks as the girls found themselves a table which was not too near anyone else. As they settled themselves down the boys came over with the drinks and Paul said, 'We have all got doubles, OK girls?'

They both laughed. 'That is fine with us. We need them after that experience.'

All of them took a long pull at their drinks, then sat there looking at each other for a while, then both girls started to say something together.

'Hold it,' said Dave, 'One at a time.'

'Go on Kath, you first.'

'I was just going to say what wonderful cities they were, just like in fairy books.'

'That is just what we said when we saw them for the first time.'

'Those cars they had, or rather flyers as he called them, I would love to have one of those. No more getting stuck in long queues, and to fly across fields and trees, fly right across the sea to Europe without getting out of the car.'

'Just a minute Jean, don't get carried away, it will be hundreds of years before that can happen.'

'Well I can dream can't I?'

Kath said, 'The men and women were beautiful.'

'Be happy with what you have sitting next to you,' said Paul giving her a gentle slap on her arm.

'Well you thought the girls were beautiful.'

'Yes, he did, especially when we saw one in the nude having a shower.'

'That settles it we want to see all of it the same as you boys have, am I right Jean?'

'You can, but not before we have seen it all the way through, there is so much we need to find out about, like when it all took place. It could have been ten thousand or a hundred thousand years ago, we are hoping for a clue as it goes along.'

'Could it have been all that long ago?' said Kath looking at them both.

'We do not know, it is something I would like to know. It was something Dave and I discussed before.'

'Let's have another drink before they close, I'll get them. Dave come and give me a hand.'

As they were walking the girls home, strung out across the road with their arms all linked together, the girls were still bubbling with excitement. Jean said, 'When can we see it again? We can come straight from work tomorrow but how I will manage to work, and think about all I have seen I don't know, and if I get any sleep tonight I will be lucky. How about you Kath?'

'I keep getting goosebumps thinking about it, if I cannot sleep tonight it will be you boys' fault, but I am glad you shared it with us. How did you get hold of it?'

'Tell you tomorrow, there is your house.'

Turning her to face him, Paul lifted up her chin giving her a gentle kiss on her lips.

'See you in the morning Jean, goodnight Dave.'

Dave and Jean said goodnight and walked on up the road.

Kath looked at Paul saying, 'If that was the best you can do, let me show you how.'

With that she kissed him long and hard. 'There, that's what I call a kiss. Now goodnight, see you tomorrow.'

CHAPTER 7

The New World

Paul and Dave entered the dining room the following morning for their breakfast, and were so engrossed discussing what they were going to do that day, they had walked up to their usual table before they realised people were already sitting there. It was a second or two before they realised it was Kath and Jean.

'What are you doing here so early? Have you come to have breakfast with us? I must say I like the idea, what do you say Paul?'

Bending over Kath and giving her a kiss, Paul said, 'Yes Dave, I would like this every morning. How about it girls?'

Kath give him a smile. 'Be careful how you say that, I may take you up on it. As to why we are here early, it is because we will not be starting our shift until two o'clock, so we are both coming to your room to see what else is on your time capsule.'

Giving Paul a wink and looking gravely at the girls Dave said, 'I don't know, we could swear them to secrecy. There is a bible in our room, what you think Paul?'

Before Paul could answer Kath gave him a slap on his arm.

'If you two have finished fooling around get your breakfast, we want to go to your room as soon as possible. And stop looking at each other that way, it is the capsule not you we want to see in your room, and you both know it. You have whetted our appetite and we are getting impatient to see more, so hurry up.'

'Alright girls, but I warn you we have a full English breakfast, so what are you going to have?'

'Just a coffee will do us, but hurry up or the morning will be gone.'

Paul beckoned the young man who was serving and asked for their breakfast with coffees all round.

Very little was said, the girls just looking out of the window pretending to interested in anything except the boys. However it was not long before their breakfast was in front of them.

Half an later they were finished with Dave saying, 'That should do me until lunch, shall we have another cup of coffee girls?'

Kath and Jean got up from the table together. 'Alright, are we going to your room or are we going home, what is it to be?'

'Come on, we want to see it as much as you girls, we are only fooling around, having a bit of fun with you.'

They all almost ran out of the dining room, the girls getting to the stairs first with the boys laughing behind them. As Paul put the key in the door he turned to the girls.

'We will have to swear you to secrecy you know.'

'I will swear you to secrecy if you don't hurry up.'

Paul laughed as he opened the door.

They all rushed in, the girls moving to the chairs as they had before, the boys setting up the capsule.

'Alright girls we will carry on from where we left it yesterday, all ready, and off we go to new wonders.'

They were again flying over North America, viewing vast orchards and fields of every kind of vegetables. There was a mixture of men, machines and robots working in them and they could also see vast low-lying buildings. There were robots and machines going in and out of them, with many kinds of transport arriving and taking off.

Joseph was all the while pointing out what was happening. Where they were passing over, he kept mentioning that in time they would be passing over deserts, but all they saw were well cultivated fields. Dave decided he would have to mention this to Paul and the girls later to see if they understood it. It was at this point that Joseph was saying,'We are now flying over the place you called Death Valley on your map, I hope you remember this later when we return over this land. You are seeing all this before the Ords came, you will see after they came and went, but as you can see it is now a valley lush with growth.'

'It can't be the Death Valley we know, look at the colours of the fruits and the trees, even the houses are bright colours. Next time we look at it we will have to fetch a camera. Why we haven't done so yet beats me. Dave, you have yours in your drawer, why not get it out now?'

'Next time, we are moving again and I don't want to miss anything.'

Kath was whispering non-stop to Jean, pointing to everything as if she could not see for herself. Both their faces were full of excitement, their eyes bright, sitting on the edges of their seats.

Kath turned to the boys. 'I feel as if I could reach out and touch everything, it is so real I feel a part of it. It's so wonderful, will we ever have a world like this?'

Dave and Paul said almost as one, 'It is the 3-D effect that makes you feel a part of it, as for whether our world will ever be like this, only time will tell, I would like to think it will.'

Joseph was talking again. 'We are now coming up to an animal reserve, one of many. They vary as to what animals are kept in them, it all depends on what part of the planet you are on. We will go lower so that you may have a closer look at them.'

Then they floated closer, almost in touching reach of some of the strangest-looking animals.

'I can't recognise hardly any of them, can you Paul? Some of them could be small dinosaurs, we will have a camera with us next time. We spent quite some time there because the reserve was so big, with so many different animals we were glad of the chance.'

Now Joseph was standing in front of them. 'You have now seen all that we had achieved. Now it has all been lost. I would like to see or know how our world, your world as it is now, has reached or passed our achievements, however that cannot be. It has been decided to leave some space on this recorder, we may have more information to add at a later time, for now this record will end.'

Suddenly Kath jumped up saying, 'Goodness, what time is it? Have we got time to have some lunch before we are due to start work?'

Paul looked at his watch. 'It's just gone half past twelve, if we hurry we can all have a bite to eat before you have to start. Switch it off Dave, we can put it away later.'

CHAPTER 8

The Proposals

It was not long before they were sitting at their table in the diner.

'What are you going to have girls?'

Jean told them to order for them while they went to the ladies' room to freshen up.

Dave noticed Kath talking to the waiter they knew as Jim. Seconds later he was at their table saying, 'Kath asked me to take your orders, because they have no time to lose, or they will miss their lunch, so what would you gentlemen like?'

They ordered roast beef for them all.

The girls had just settled down when their meals arrived. Jim served the girls first saying, 'Is there anything else I can get you ladies?' giving them a mocking bow.

Kath picked up on his fooling by saying, 'Yes, my good man, can you fetch me some English mustard? Be quick about it before my lunch gets cold.'

Placing the rest of the meals on the table he said, 'I will be but a moment with your mustard my lady,' giving her a quick bow.

They all laughed as Jim came back with a large tin of mustard placing it in front of Kath.

'Oh Jim you are a devil.'

Giving Kath a big grin he pulled a proper mustard pot from behind his back while picking up the tin he had placed in front of her. Giving another bow he left them.

Jean said, 'Jim was full of himself. I have never seen him like that before, still we do not see him that much because we are on different shifts.'

They all settled down to eat their meals, with very little being said until they had finished when Dave said, 'Now tonight when you have finished work we will have a quick drink, then go for a walk and not watch the capsule, OK girls?'

'No, it is not OK. We will watch the capsule for an hour or so first, we can go for a walk later. Come on Kath it is time we got ready for our shift, see you later boys if you are good.'

'Well Dave, talk about getting hooked on something. Those girls most certainly have, it looks as if our romantic nights are over.'

'Oh no they are not, we will have to put our foot down. We will watch it for an hour then we are out of it, a drink then a trip to the park. Right, all in favour put your hands up.'

They laughed as they put both hands up.

'Let's go to the bar, it looks as if we have time on our hands until the girls get off work, we have got a good six hours to pass. Any ideas, and don't say we can drink it away, I want a clear head for tonight. I am going to ask Kath to come over to Leeds to meet my parents. It is no good, I have fallen for her, hook, line and sinker.'

'Paul I think we should get to the bar, then we have some serious talking to do, come on.'

They went though to the dining room, waving to the girls who were at the far side tidying the tables. Having ordered some drinks they looked around, and spotting an empty table near the window, made their way there carrying the drinks.

'Yes, this should do us Dave.'

They sat down sipping their drinks, both deep in thought.

It was Dave who broke the silence, looking up at Paul. 'What do you mean about asking Kath to come to Leeds, do you mean to meet your parents? You have only known her for a few days, it is a serious step. Besides you have never taken a girl home before.'

'I know that. Anyway you said you felt the same way about Jean, and that was after the first night. Anyway I have made up my mind she is the girl for me. Hell, what if she says no, and feels different about me? I really have fallen in love. Bloody hell, me in love, that is a turn up for the books. I have not even met her parents yet, what if they don't like me?'

'Stop, you are rambling now, just calm down, I feel the same way about Jean, but I was thinking about coming up here on weekends. That way we could get to know them better and they could do the same. We could take our time and get to know their parents, then they could come to meet ours.'

'No, I must ask her right now. Look after my drink I am going to find her, I must know how she feels about me.'

'Wait, it is no good you rushing in like a bull in a china shop, we need to talk this. Just calm down. You will frighten her to death, rushing in the way you are. Here, drink up, while I go and get us topped up, wait there until I come back.'

Dave got up quickly before Paul could object, rushed to the bar and ordered two large whiskies looking back to see if Paul was still sat at the table. Giving a sigh he saw that he was still there.

Arriving back at the table, he said, 'There, get on the outside of that, and start thinking straight. Cheers, down the hatch.'

Paul laughed. 'Yes, down the hatch, thanks for calming me down, but I am going to marry her if it's the last thing I do, and I will not take no for an answer. When we meet the girls for a drink before we go to our room tonight, give me a few minutes alone with her and I will sound her out.'

'Alright, now let us go for a walk before we get too drunk to go anywhere tonight. We can go to the park for starters and on the way back we can call into the village shop and get a box of chocolates. That should sweeten the girls.'

'That's a brilliant idea, we will do that. I wonder what kind Kath likes, soft or hard centres? There I go, saying I want to marry her and I don't know her likes and dislikes.'

'Yes Paul, and that works both ways, what does Kath know about your likes and dislikes? Now do you see why I keep saying, go easy and let us all get to know each other better before you rush her off her feet.'

They were now well into the park taking the route to the lake, neither of them realising where they were, until they found themselves on the edge of the lake. They stood there for a while looking across the water, seeing nothing, both deep in thought, then without a word they both sat down. Paul sat with his knees up to his chin, hands grasped together over them. Dave sat stretched out with one leg straight and the other bent up, his left hand shading his eyes as he looked across the water.

Several minutes went by before: 'Dave, you are right you know, we do need to learn a lot more about the girls, and them about us, but I am still going to tell her how I feel. I must know how she feels about me. Do you remember Charlie, he used to be our third cashier who got moved to that new branch? Now I know what he was going through with his girlfriend, I used to laugh at him, and come to think about it, some of the stupid advice I gave him, I hope he didn't take any notice of me. He used to tell me, wait until I fell in love. I would not know what hit me. How right he was.'

'Knowing Charlie, he had a mind of his own, so I don't think he would have taken too much notice of what you said to him, just like you. Are you going to take notice of everything I tell you?'

'Well maybe not everything, but at least you are making me think more carefully. I could have blown everything if you hadn't stopped me. You are a good friend Dave, and I do take notice. We've just proved it. Here I am sitting quietly discussing how I feel and what to do about it and now I have more or less decided what I am going to do. How about you and Jean? You said you feel about her like I feel about Kath. Are you going to invite her to meet your parents?'

'Of course I want to; I am going to suggest that I come back as often as I can on weekends, then invite her to Leeds. Wait until you have had a word with Kath, I have an idea it will take everything out of my hands. Those girls are good friends and what one will do the other may do. Wait and see what happens tonight, somehow I think we will be giving the capsule a miss tonight.'

Paul looked at his watch. 'Do you know what time it is, it's half past four. By the time we call in the shop for the chocolates and get tidied up it will be time for dinner and the girls. I bet they are wondering where we are. Come on, let's make a move.'

As they wandered their way back through the park very little was said. They were both in a world of their own and now and again one of them would grin to himself at some secret thought. It was not until they were passing the shop that either noticed where they were, then Dave touched Paul's arm.

'Here we are. Come on, let's see what they can tempt us with.'

As they entered the shop they noticed an elderly lady with glasses perched on the end of her nose. She looked up at them giving them a toothy smile.

'Now then Sirs. What can I do for you?'

'Chocolates, have you got any fancy boxes please?' Paul grinned at Dave while looking around.

'Right behind you in the corner.'

They both moved to the corner and were surprised by the assortment; there were big and small boxes, some with fancy ribbons.

'You have a nice selection.'

Dave had picked one of the big ones with a pink ribbon, Paul meanwhile held two big ones in his hands. 'Which do you think Dave, the this one with the blue ribbon or the one with the white?'

'That with the big white one looks good. It's your choice, which do you think?'

'Alright, the white one, they have a good assortment.'

They bought some fancy wrapping paper and Dave asked the

woman if she would wrap them up. She was all the time adjusting her glasses, they kept slipping down her nose and after wrapping them she put the boxes of chocolates in a carrier bag.

'I am sure your young ladies will like them.'

Once back in their room they both had a quick shower and had a complete change of clothes. Feeling quite pleased with what they saw in the mirror they made their way to the bar for a quick drink before dinner.

Once at the bar Paul ordered a whisky for both of them saying, 'We are both going to need this.'

'No we don't need it yet. We will not be seeing the girls until eight o'clock, it is only six-thirty now.'

'I know that. Go on get it down you, we can always get another when we meet them, anyway I need one now to keep my calm. Hell, I know I will make a pig's ear of it when I see Kath, I have already forgotten how and what I was going to tell her.'

'You will be OK. Just think about the lake and what we decided, not to rush it, just sound her out. Everything is going to be fine. If you get into trouble give me a nod I'll come over. I know you won't, but it will make it you feel better, to know that I will be on hand. So drink up let's see what they can tempt us with for dinner tonight.'

They both slowly sipped their whiskies, Dave looking around.

'Jean is watching us, let's finish the drinks and go to our table. You can do without another drink so leave the barman where he is.'

So saying Dave got up, moving towards the table. After a second or two Paul followed him, but Jean beat him to the table.

'Come slowcoach, don't you want any dinner tonight?'

'Well funny you say that, but I not sure I feel like it.'

'You are not ill are you?' said Jean, putting her hand on his brow. 'You do feel hot.'

'He is alright, we will both have chicken tonight. And can we have a small bottle of white wine to go with it?'

Looking a bit concerned she wrote down their order. 'Aright if you are sure I can't get you anything else.'

Giving her a smile and a wink, Paul said, 'I am alright, now hurry up with our dinners.'

Smiling back at him she skipped away.

'Did you notice she still skips away?'

Paul gave Dave a grin saying, 'I must pull my socks up, mustn't get her worried, must I?'

An hour later they had both finished their meal.

'Well Jean looked pleased that you ate all your dinner, she looks her own happy self again. Come on we will see if we can find our usual table in the bar room.'

Having ordered and collected their drinks they found that their usual table was free. Hardly had they sat down when the girls appeared to join them, Jean saying, 'We finished a few minutes early so here we are. Don't get up Paul I will get this round in. Do you boys need a top up while I am at it?'

'Kath, I will give you a hand.'

Putting her hand on his shoulder she gave him a gentle push. 'We will manage, don't forget we are used to it.'

Giving a big smile she skipped away to the bar and when they came back Paul said, 'To that corner table with me. I have something I need to tell you.'

Looking a bit startled she followed him. Then, sitting down facing him Kath said, 'What is the matter, you look so serious?'

Leaning towards her he caught her hands in his, then blurted out, 'Kath I am in love with you and I want you to meet my parents. Tell me you feel the same way.'

Kath recoiled. 'Oh you, I thought you where going to tell me something terrible, like you did not want to see me, or you were married or something. I like you a lot but we have only just met, I need time to get to know you better, and you me, as for meeting your parents, yes, of course I want to, but maybe you should meet mine first.'

'Yes, of course I want to meet your parents, shall we go now tonight?'

'No, you still have nearly a week before you go home, let's keep it like it is for now. I will prepare my parents first; as it is they will have a fit if I tell them I want to go to Leeds to meet your parents, having just met you.'

Meanwhile Dave was saying much the same thing to Jean. It was not what he had planned, but like Paul he could not keep how he felt about her to himself. Jean said much the same thing to Dave as Kath had to Paul, except she was more excited than Kath and might have agreed to take Dave to meet her parents there and then, if Kath and Paul had not rejoined them.

Dave looked at them both. 'Well, what is happening then, and before you ask I have told Jean that I want to see a lot more of her, and I will be coming back as often as I can, and some day soon I hope. Come on you two, out with it. What are you doing?'

'I don't think we will go to your room tonight to watch the capsule, let us have another drink then go for a walk, we appear to all have a lot to talk about.'

'Good idea, I will get them. Another lager for you Paul?'

'Yes but I will have a whisky chaser, I need it badly.'

'Oh, you poor boy. Anyway I feel like a double as well, get the same for Jean.'

Later in the park they took their separate paths, agreeing they would meet later, Paul saying they would come and find them.

Paul and Kath said little to each other until they were sat beside the lake again. Paul had his arm around Kath's shoulders, then turning her to face him give her a light kiss on the cheek.

'Well, come on my love, put me out of my misery. Do you feel the same. Do you love me, or could you love me?'

'I could not have answered you yesterday, but you telling me how you feel has made me realise I do feel the same. But let's get to know each other more first. I never thought that it would happen like this, so quick. I liked you from that first time you came in for your dinner, but for you to fall in love with me so quickly, you take my breath away.'

'That is all I wanted to hear you say, that you love me.' With that he jumped up shouting, 'Yes, yes, and a thousand times yes.'

'Sit down silly, someone will hear you and think you are mad.'

'I want the world to know,' said Paul, pulling her into his arms. They both laughed as they kissed and Kath threw her arms his neck. With that Paul swung her around and around until they both fell down. They cuddled where they fell, laughing and kissing and at that moment they were in a world of their own.

Later as the moment passed and they lay in each other's arms, Kath suddenly said, 'Yes, you must meet my parents, I will arrange for you to come to tea tomorrow, I think they will be both in. Can you come to my house at six o'clock sharp?'

'Yes, yes of course I will. By the way, what is your Dad like, do you think he will like me?'

Kath laughed saying. 'Mum will adore you, Dad will be alright when you tell him you work in a bank. Have you bought a suit with you? It would make a good impression with him. He likes men in suits, he is a bit of a snob in his own way.'

'No I did not have room for one in my backpack, shall I fetch one with me next time and meet him then?'

'You are meeting him tomorrow, suit or no suit. I am glad you said you are coming back again, good job for you,' she said, giving him a slap and kiss.

'Come, let us go and find Jean and Dave and see how they have got on. Jean is already besotted with him you know, it must be fate you two coming here as friends and Jean and I being such good friends. It is good, I hope we all will be friends always. By the way, when we get close to them we must make a noise.'

'Now why is that I wonder?'

They both laughed as Kath gave his arm a squeeze.

They joined the path that Dave and Jean had gone up and as they turned a curve in the path the path, they started to sing.

'Not so loud, you will wake the dead with that voice.'

Paul picked up a piece of dead wood and started to hit the bushes, and they both laughed.

As they were coming up to another curve in the path, Dave and Jean were coming towards them with Jean swinging on Dave's arm. They were both grinning from ear to ear, looking into each other's bright shining eyes.

Seeing them Jean gave a wave of her hand, and leaving Dave she ran up to them both and flinging her arms around them both, panted out, 'We are engaged and going for the ring tomorrow, it is wonderful!'

When Jean had disentangled herself from them, Kath said, 'I believe we are. Well are we?'

'Yes, of course we are.'

Both girls hugged each other, with tears in their eyes.

Dave coming up to them said, 'Hey, it is nothing to cry over. I hope not anyway.'

Grasping Paul's hand, he added, 'Congratulations Paul.'

'To both of you too, come on back to the bar, we have something to celebrate.'

They all linked arms together, it was a tight squeeze along the narrow paths as they skipped and danced, laughing and singing.

Arriving back at the hotel bar, Paul called out, 'A bottle of champagne barman, with four glasses if you please,' adding, 'Go on girls find us a table, Dave take the glasses.' Paying the barman Paul added, 'Just got ourselves engaged, it is great.'

As the barman went to the cash register he spoke to the

manager, who nodded his head.

Coming back to Paul, the barman said, 'They are two of our girls, Kath and Jean. Well, the manager said the champagne is on the house with our compliments and best wishes.'

Back at the table, Paul told them, 'With the compliments of the management, ladies.'

After filling their glasses they faced the bar and raised them in a salute.

'That was good of them, Paul. Now that you have told them it will be all around the hotel tomorrow.'

'Is there an early bus into Leeds tomorrow girls?'

'Paul, you are not going home are you?'

'No Kath, but I thought that if all your workmates get to know you have become engaged, you should have a ring to show them. What do you say Dave?'

'Yes, it is a must. Well is there a bus in the morning or not girls?'

Both girls answered almost together, 'Yes, but it is early at seven o'clock.'

'OK. Seven o'clock it is. I know there is one arriving from Leeds at twelve-thirty, so we can be back before you have start work.'

Paul nodded to Dave. 'Come on Dave, let us get some more drinks in.'

They both got up, went to the bar and ordered their drinks.

'Well Dave we have done it now, my Mum and Dad are in for a shock. You know what my Mum will say, you are too young yet to get that serious with a girl, what are you thinking of? Yes, I can just imagine her. What about your parents, think what they will say. Going on holiday, coming back engaged to girl they have never met, it will be a shock for them.'

'Oh, I will get much the same as you I expect. Anyway nothing will stop me now, but I never thought things would go this fast. Talk about being swept off one's feet and I did it myself. Look at the girls, heads together. I wonder what they are saying as if we didn't know. They don't seem to be missing us at the moment, let us get a whisky before we go back with the drinks, I need one.' With that Dave called for two whiskies.

'It did not take long for us to finish off that bottle of champagne did it? Mind you the girls had more than their share, sipping it almost between each word they spoke.'

'I doubt if they knew what they were doing, they were that excited. When we have finished these drinks I think we had better take them home. Come on let's get back to them.'

'Here we are girls, did you miss us?'

Both of them looked up showing a mouthful of teeth as they smiled, Kath saying, 'No, have you been somewhere?'

'There, you see Dave? I told you they were not interested in us, just our money. Come on Dave let's go.'

Kath grabbed his arm saying, 'Not so fast, you are not getting away from me that easy.'

She pulled him into his chair and gave him a big kiss, Jean did the same with Dave, putting her arms around his neck and saying, 'You are mine for always,' as Dave gave her a kiss.

They sat there for another hour, the girls asking to know more about their parents, laughing at something one of them said, until Dave got up.

'I think it is time to take you girls home. Finish off your drinks, we have to be up early in the morning.'

Laughing together they got up and made their way to the door calling out goodnight to the barman. As he waved to them Kath and Jean blew him a kiss.

They walked the girls home, and after saying their goodnights, strolled back to the hotel. Back in their room, Paul picked up the phone and asked for an early call for six o'clock.

'I am glad you remembered to do that Paul, I didn't even think of it, not that I will get much sleep tonight. What sort of ring are you going to get?'

'Go to sleep, or at least keep quiet and let me.'

The following morning after getting their early call, they

dressed, went downstairs and managed to get a drink of coffee with some toast.

Getting to the bus stop they were surprised to see the girls there.

'Hello Kath what are you two doing here this early?'

'Well how do you both know what size rings to get, you don't know our sizes.'

'Good heavens, we never thought of that. Will that mean you are coming in with us?'

'Of course we are, you want us to, don't you?'

'What a daft question, we cannot do without you. After all it is your fingers that need the rings.'

Going close to her Paul gave her a gentle hug. 'You should have suggested it last night, even if you had not been going for the rings, it would have been a nice bus ride out for us all.'

'It was Jean's idea that we came with you, she rang me last night and while we were talking it dawned on us that you didn't know our sizes. Neither did we, that is why we are here instead of telephoning you last night. It is a shame that we cannot make a full day of it, we have to work this afternoon. Hold on I have an idea. I won't be long just make sure the bus waits for me.'

Then she was gone. Paul and Dave noticed that she had gone to the hotel and wondered why. It was a good ten minutes before Kath came running back, the bus had pulled up just as she came up to them. Getting on the bus and having settled in their seats, Kath breathlessly explained that she had arranged for the morning shift girls to cover by doing their afternoon shift, beaming all over her face.

'I hope it is alright with everyone, but I did not have time to explain what I had in mind.'

'You are an angel, right Dave?'

'Too right, now we can have plenty of time, we will not have to rush into the first shop. This is going to be great, we can have lunch then maybe go to the pictures or something.'

Turning to Jean, Kath said, 'We must ring our families, they will be expecting us back for work this afternoon. It will have to be the first thing to do when we get to Leeds, because I am sure Mum said she is going out this morning.'

Jean nodded agreement, both Paul and Dave nodded together.

'Yes, of course you must, it will save any worry. I must say Dave, the girls are full of ideas today. Two bright ones and so early in the morning, there must be a third one coming up.'

They all laughed together, the girls putting their arms through the boys' and giving them a squeeze of pleasure.

With a lot of banter and happy talk they arrived in Leeds. Helping the girls off the bus, Paul and Dave looked around.

'Come on this way, I know a nice refreshment bar where we can have a bit to eat and a soft drink. You know the one Paul, just before Woolworth's. It is nice in there, we can top up our breakfast, that piece of toast didn't do much for me.'

'OK with me, and I am sure the girls would enjoy something as well.'

'Lead on Dave.' Jean waved her arm as she put the other one though his.

Later as they strolled up the road gazing in the shop windows, Paul stopped.

'Let's cross over. I remember seeing a good jewellers up that side street, I am sure it is that one. Come on there's a crossing and the traffic has stopped.'

They ran the few yards to it and made it across. Going up the side street they came to the jewellers, stopping outside.

'If we can't find what we want in here there are plenty more shops we can look in.'

The girls were busy looking in the window, first pointing at one ring then another with 'Oh, that's nice, and that one.'

Finally Dave caught hold of Jean saying, 'You will be able to see them better inside.'

Gently he led her through the door with Kath and Paul

following them. Going up to the young man behind the counter, Dave asked if he would show them some engagement rings.

Putting his arm under the glass counter he pulled out first one tray then another.

'Would the young ladies like to look at these? If there is one that you like let me know.'

'Can you check both of our sizes please. Come on Kath you first.'

Having checked and told him their sizes, he said, 'When you see one you like I can get it in your size.'

Having had a good long look, Jean said, 'We saw some that we liked in the window, can we see them?'

'Would you like to come to the window and show me which tray?'

Both girls went out side and pointed to the ones they liked.

Coming back inside he had the two trays on the counter.

'If you would like to show me which ones I will check the sizes for you.'

Kath immediately picked up one with two small diamonds either side of a ruby, and putting it on her finger turned to Paul.

'Do you like it?' she asked, looking into his eyes.

'If you like it that is all that matters,' he replied.

Giving him a kiss, she said, 'I love it, it's not too much is it?'

'Not if it is the one you want.'

Jean held out her finger to Kath, 'Do you like it Kath?'

Kath saw that Jean had picked one with two small diamonds on either side of a larger one.

Both girls threw their arms around each other, with tears of happiness in their eyes.

'Now look what you have done Dave, you have made them cry.'

Breaking their embrace they threw their arms around the boys.

'Take it easy, we are in company Kath, save this for later.'

'Don't be silly. There will never be another time like this, this is one day I will always remember.'

The young man asked them if they wanted them back in the boxes.

Jean looked again at hers. 'I never want to take it off, but I want you to give it to me properly Dave, so I will have it in its box please.'

With another long look at it, she took it off, giving it back to the young man.

Kath gave hers back after flashing it at Paul again and giving him a kiss on his cheek.

Paul and Dave gave the young man their plastic cards.

As they got outside the shop Paul saw a taxi cab coming up the road, putting up his hand he hailed it. As it pulled up alongside them, he said, 'Come on, we have somewhere to go.'

Leaning into the cab he said to the driver, 'Roundhay Park please.'

When they were all in, he added, 'Before you ask, just wait and see; it is only a short ride.'

Within minutes they were at the park. Paul paid the taxi, and turning to Dave said, 'Right you two can both take that path, Kath and I will take this one. I am going to propose to this young lady and I think Kath and I would like to be alone for it.'

'What more surprises are you going to come up with today? But I think if we find a quiet spot we can do it altogether. We are all close friends, besides it will make it different and more to remember this day by. Come on, shall we?'

Looking at Dave, Paul replied, 'Let's go for it.'

Linking arms they walked deeper into the park, until they came to a wall with a park bench set back. As they sat down Dave blushed.

'I feel daft with you two here as well.'

Paul looked at Dave then got down one knee in front of

Kath. Taking the ring out of its box, he caught hold of her left hand and looking up her said, 'Kathleen Williams, will you marry me?'

'Yes, I will marry you Paul.'

With a grin a mile wide he put the ring on her finger and leaning forward he held her face in his hands as he give her a long lingering kiss.

Dave was already down on one knee himself, holding Jean's hand.

'Jean Brown, will you do me the honour of becoming my wife?'

Leaning forward she kissed him.

'I will, yes I will.'

Dave slipped the ring on her finger and with that she went down on her knees, and grasping his face in her hands she looked into his eyes kissing him as if she would never let go. When she did, Dave managed to gasp out, 'I will have some more of that later.'

They all stood up, looked at each other and laughing linked arms. They had only walked a few yards like it when Paul stopped.

'If you do not mind, I would like to walk with my future wife on my own.'

So saying, he unhooked Kath's arm from Jean's, walking quickly ahead with Kath.

'See you later in about half an hour by the gate we came in by, OK?' Waving his arm above his head Paul turned up a side path with Kath.

Later, having met up again they stood discussing what to do next. Kath was standing in front of Paul.

'Let us do something special, I want this it to be a day to remember for always, so it must be something none of us have done before. Come on, think, what would be something that we have all not done before?'

After coming up with ideas such as dinner at some posh

restaurant or going to the cinema among other things, Dave said,

'There is something that I have often thought about, but I've never got around to. You know about the old-fashioned music hall show Paul, well it is showing at the theatre. Have any of you seen it?'

Jean and Kath said they had never seen it and they would love to, it would be something new and different for all of them.

Paul laughed, 'That is a great idea, it is something I have never been to either. I have seen it on TV and often thought about it. Let's go and see if we can get some tickets for tonight and find out what time it starts and finishes, we don't want to miss the last bus back. By the way girls, what is the time of the last one?'

Kath looked at Jean. 'The last one leaves here at nine-ten on a weekday, I am sure that will be too early for us. I wonder if there is a matinee today.'

Looking at his watch Paul ran to the road and looking up and down saw a taxi. He waved his hand, and as luck would have it, it was empty and pulled over for them. He asked the driver to take them to the theatre and they all got in.

When they got there Dave walked up to the booking office. Their luck was in again. It was open and there was a matinee that day, starting in two hours' time. By now Paul had joined him and butting in asked if there were any seats. The girl said there were some at the back and one box left.

'We will have the box please. OK Dave, our luck is in today,' Paul remarked as he paid for the tickets with his bank card.

'I will square up with you later, now let's get back to the girls with the good news, I am looking forward to it. Boy, what a day and it is not over yet.'

Going back to the girls, waving the tickets in the air, Paul said, 'We have a two hour wait so let us go for a drink in that pub we just passed.'

Paul leading the way with Kath, they made their way to the pub, where they found themselves a seat by the window.

'Right I will get the drinks in. You girls fancy a lager?'

'Just a half,' they both said and Paul asked for the same. Dave left them and went to the bar, coming back in a few minutes with a tray of drinks and putting the tray on the table.

'Help yourselves everyone. By the way they serve meals here, shall we have something now?'

They all agreed as Paul passed around the menu.

An hour later they made their way back to the theatre, noticing there were quite a lot of people going in. Joining the small queue in front of them they made their way in, there was a notice pointing upstairs to the boxes. Seeing their number pointing to the right they followed the signs.

Arriving at the entrance to their box, Paul drew back the curtains a bit wider as he let them all in. Following them he closed the curtain, and sat with Kath.

Kath and Jean were leaning forward looking at everyone around them.

'I have never been in here before, have you Kath? Actually I have never been in a theatre at all before, look at all the colour. Look at the people; some of them have old-fashioned hats on, and shawls, some of them are dressed in old-fashioned dresses as well, it's wonderful.'

Paul pulled on Dave's arm and beckoning him to follow got up saying, 'We will not be long girls, back in a few minutes.'

'Come downstairs Dave, I saw where they were getting those hats from.'

Once downstairs Paul led Dave to the other side of the foyer. There they saw two girls giving hats and shawls to people. Going up to them Paul asked if they could buy a hat or something, and with a laugh she said, 'No Sir, they are free, but we will want them back after the show. Now what would you like?' picking up a big hat with feathers on it.

'Go on Dave, get one for Jean.'

Dave picked up one that had a big bunch of berries on it. They both said thank you and ran back up the stairs, and going into the box they put the hats on the girls' heads. There were squeals of delight from them as they placed them on properly. Looking at each other they laughed, and turning to Paul and Dave they kissed them both.

'Oh, how wonderful, I really feel part of it already Kath.'

Just then the music started to play.

Later coming out of the theatre, Jean said. 'I am hungry. Can we get something to eat?'

'I think we will could all do with something, it as been quite a while since lunch. There is a good restaurant not far from here I know about, we can try it, come on.'

Laughing about some of the performances they had seen, and repeating some of the jokes, it was not long before they arrived at the restaurant.

They walked in and found themselves a table with the help of one of the waiters. As they sat down Kath whispered, 'This looks expensive, we could get some fish and chips.'

'What, not today, this is a special day, our engagement. We don't want fish and chips on a day like this thank you.'

It was another ten minutes before they were ready to order. The girls were excitedly discussing the musical acts, with Paul and Dave managing to put a word in now and again, but the waiter did eventually manage to get their order.

After they had all eaten their meal, both the girls said they had enjoyed it and that it had been something special, and what a perfect way to end the day. Finishing off their second bottle of wine, Jean looked her watch, saying, 'If we go now we can catch the earlier bus, I don't want to leave it to the last one.' They all agreed and the girls said they would meet them at the door as they were going to the ladies' room. Paul and Dave said alright as they had to settle the bill.

As they were waiting for the girls, Dave said, 'Well we certainly pushed the boat out today Paul, I hope there is enough left in to pay the hotel bill.'

'You have no need to worry. I have a fair bit saved up, I will see you alright.'

Just then the girls came back and they hurried to the bus station.

In the bus they were all in high spirits; giggling and laughing together they were back in their village before they realised it.

Back at the hotel they found themselves an empty table. Paul and Dave went to the bar for the drinks, as they gave the girls their drinks they were both smothered with kisses. Gasping for air they asked, 'What was that for?'

Laughing together Jean said, 'For making this such a wonderful day, Kath and I will never forget it.'

Two hours and many drinks later, they walked the girls home and said their lingering goodnights.

Arriving back at the hotel they found the bar was still open.

'Come on Dave, let us finish a great day with a good liqueur, what do you say?'

They both walked up to the bar. After a bit of debating with the barman they settled for whiskey liqueur, took their drinks and sat down at a table. They spent an hour recounting the day with many a laugh.

'Well Dave, the girls said it had been a day they would never forget, I think I can safely say the same; a holiday I will never forget. First we found the time capsule, then met the girls, got engaged, went to a music hall show, what more could we ask for?'

'Yes, I agree Paul, it's been a dream holiday, but we should ring our parents and tell them we have met some nice girls. At least it will prepare them a bit. I don't think we should tell them that we have got engaged yet, that will be shock to them when we do, so let's give them some warning,'

'Yes, I had not given them any thought, it's too late now but first thing tomorrow. I can just hear Mum, she will say, "That is nice dear," then she will want to know all about her. It will not be easy trying to be casual about it, as you know she is always on to me to find a nice girl. When I take Kath home to meet her it will make her day.'

'I know what you mean, but it will be my Dad with me. "Now don't go rushing into things son," I can just hear him saying it.'

'Let's finish our drinks and get to bed.'

CHAPTER 9

The Unbelievable

Next morning Dave and Paul were surprised to see the girls sat at their table.

'What are you two doing here so early, did we make any arrangement to meet up?'

Jean pulled Dave to her, giving him a kiss. 'Good morning to you too. Is this the way you are going to treat your fiancée when you greet her? What are you doing here, you don't think we are going to miss the rest of the story on that capsule do you?'

Paul and Kath kissed each other good morning as the waiter came over, but before he could ask for their order Jean flashed her ring at him.

'I got engaged yesterday. So did Kath, show him your ring.'

'Well congratulations to you both, that was quick work. What have you lads got that I haven't?'

Paul looked at the waiter. 'I will have the full English breakfast, what about you Dave? And you girls, are you going to join us?'

They had a little confab together and said they would have the same.

As the waiter went away Kath said, 'Bill is a bit of a rogue really. He has asked us both to go out with him at one time and another, and we are both friends of his wife, and he has two children'

'It takes all kinds to make a world, but you have nothing to worry about Kath, I am a one-woman man with eyes only for you.'

'You had better be.'

After having enjoyed a good breakfast they went up to the room, there they set up the capsule and took their seats. Looking around with his finger poised above the button Dave said, 'Here we go, what wonders will we see today?'

As they watched, Joseph appeared saying, 'Now I am going to show you the after-effects, which will, I am sure, upset you, but I feel I must prepare you for it. We will begin by retracing our journey over America.

As they approached the land mass, he said, 'First we will go along just inland from the coast where you saw the main settlements,' and now all they could see were the beaches which appeared to go on for miles inland. They heard Joseph speaking again, 'You will notice that there are no buildings or trees for a long way inland, they were all disintegrated along with the people that lived there.' They went lower, skimming over the land; there was not a thing to suggest that there had been people and houses here.

'Now,' said Joseph, 'we will go across from east to west, I will point out the places where the big cities were, where the biggest loss of life and building was.' Going further inland they passed over many areas of bare land which they had not noticed before. Joseph was saying, 'We are now coming up to one of the largest inland cities, one which we visited on the way here before. Look hard below us, you named it as Death Valley on your map, a most appropriate name now.'

All they could see was what appeared to be the remains of a pyramid, the rest of the land was just barren waste for miles. It was just a desert now with hills in the distant, no people or animals.

Jean gasped out, 'I remember that city, full of those beautiful houses and people. How could anyone destroy such beauty?'

'Shall we turn it off, if it is going to upset you Jean? Maybe we should.'

'No, I will be alright for now.'

Meanwhile they were still moving, passing over more deserts

where there had been people and houses. There were no longer the vast orchards of fruits that had looked so fresh and colourful, but barren waste as far as eye could see. Now they were flying over a mountain range and Joseph was speaking again.

'We are now going to look in some of the caves. Most of our people sheltered in these natural or man-made ones thoughout the planet. What you are going to see will be very stressful and horrifying, but you need to know what happened to us.'

Now they were looking at the inside of a large cave. At first they did not notice anything but as they went deeper in they saw them, men, women and children, sitting, standing or laying down as though sleeping.

They all looked so natural, but they were all dead, Joseph was saying, 'We do not know how they did this, we believe the oxygen was taken away by the rays, even out of their bodies, which would have mummified them. Their blood is just dust in their bodies, by their postures they must have died instantly. We are sealing as many caves as we can, but we have more urgent problems to deal with. We will continue with our journey around the planet.'

They did not continue flying, but just appeared over different parts of the planet. It was in Britain that they saw the tunnels that had been made as shelters. Somewhere in the south they hovered above a square hole in the ground, then they saw inside. The roof appeared to be large flat rock and the tunnel itself had recesses. It was in these that they saw the bodies, all looking like the ones seen in the caves, mummified. The tunnel appeared to be very long with an exit at the end.

Joseph's voice in the background was keeping up a running commentary, 'There were many parts of the planet that could only use the tunnel system, not everyone who used them died, many were sealed using their own supply of oxygen, the lack of it was something that had been unforeseen.'

Paul reached across, switching off the capsule. 'We have seen enough for today, it has not only upset the girls but I have had it for now. What say we go for a drink to calm us all down?'

Both the girls had handkerchiefs to their eyes, as they nodded their agreement.

They put the capsule away under the bed as usual and both Paul and Dave with their arms around the girls, made their way downstairs to the bar. The girls went to their table while Paul and Dave got the drinks. Back at the table Dave handed the girls their drinks.

'Here you are, I got us all a strong drink each, I think we need one.'

They sat there in silence for a while, no one wanting to speak, just sipping their drinks. Finally Kath suggested they go home to freshen up for work, and they would see them later.

When the girls had gone, Paul went and got the drinks in. Coming back to the table and sitting down he looked at Dave.

'I think it was a bit too much for the girls this time. Mind you it was upsetting for all of us, it was worse than the last war, not that we were there but we have both seen films of it. Think how long ago that must have happened. I wonder if we will ever know how many thousands of years ago it was?'

'When you think about it, it shows you what man can overcome, they had to restart from the beginning twice, first time when they were put here, then this last time. I reckon we are a resilient lot when you think about it Paul.'

'I hadn't thought of it, but you are right. What a way to go though, after building up such a beautiful world. Like the girls said, I hope this world will achieve it one day. Maybe our children's, children's children will. I hope so, it must be great to live in a world like that.'

'Just had another thought, I wonder about those mummies that they are finding around the world, you know it's been in the papers a lot about them, I wonder if they are anything to do with what we have watching.'

'Doubt it, if they are then there must be something wrong with the carbon dating.'

'They could be wrong Paul, anything is possible, scientists have been wrong before you know. Look at the archaeologists, look how wrong they have been, by what we have seen from the capsule they are way off the mark.'

'There you go again. Don't you think that bit about black men being the original inhabitants is enough; that on its own will cause pandemonium. Mind you when you think about it, of the four main races in the world, three of them had civilisation long before the blacks. In the evolution of man it explains why the big difference, why the black man was still a primitive race in most of the world, although he is proving to be just intelligent as everyone else. Makes you wonder how right the historians and the archaeologists are. When all this gets out they will all be on our backs, the more I think about it, the more I think we should put it back where we found it.'

'You cannot mean that, but we can keep it to ourselves for a while yet. Wait until something else happens to suggest there maybe an older civilisation than what is thought.'

'Anyway it is time for us to freshen up before lunch, so let's go.'

CHAPTER 10

Surprise

After they had freshened up, Dave and Paul made their way to the diner, the girls were already there as they expected. They sat down at their usual table and it was not long before Jean came to them, giving them both a smile.

'Yes, Sirs what would you like, can I take your orders?'

'Tell you what I would like Miss, but it is not on the menu.' whispered Dave.

'Behave yourself or I will have to fetch the manager.'

'Come on you two, let's order lunch before blows are struck. Anyway how are you both?'

'Well it was upsetting, but we are alright now. I have not time to talk now, so what would you like for lunch?'

Paul picked the chicken pie, Dave said, he would have the lamb.

Later when Jean bought their dessert, she said, 'We have some news for you both, we will tell you tonight so no asking what it is.'

Giving her little skip she was gone.

After they had finished their lunch they went to the bar and got a drink each which they took to the table by the window. Sitting there they reviewed what they had seen and heard from the capsule until Paul said, 'I wish we could be watching it this afternoon instead of sitting here, I wonder how much more there is.'

'Well why not watch it tonight with the girls, we could go into Leeds on the next bus. If we hurry we can catch it, collect our car and be back in time to meet the girls.'

'OK, I am with you, let's go.'

They both took another sip of their drinks and rushed out, as they got out of the hotel the bus passed them. Running hard they got to the bus stop just in time to be the last ones on.

'Made it,' Paul gasped as they sat down. 'I think we need to do more exercise,' he grinned.

'You could be right.'

'Let's not tell the girls tonight about the car, they don't know we have one, we can surprise them in the morning.'

The rest of the journey they discussed where they could take the girls and in the end they decided to wait to see if there somewhere the girls would like to go, or do.

Fortunately the garage where they kept the car was in the next street to where they lived. Thinking that it would be better not to go home, where they would have to explain everything, they decided to go straight to the garage, pick up the car and drive back to the hotel, then they would have time to get tidied up before dinner.

Having picked up the car they decided to fill it up with petrol in town, noticing that it was quite a bit cheaper than in the village. Driving back, Paul who was driving, remarked that it was going to take them less than half the time it had taken on the bus. Arriving at the hotel they parked the car in the front not far from the main entrance.

Going to their room they freshened up and went down for dinner. As they passed the kitchen door Kath was standing there and as they came up to her she whispered to Paul 'See you later lover boy.'

With a little wave she was gone. Paul grinned at Dave. 'Well some us of have it, others don't.'

Going to the bar they got their drinks, as they got to their table Jean was waiting for them.

'You are late, we have not seen you all day. We missed you.'

They both grinned and give her a wink.

'What have you been up to, something that is for sure. I can see it in your faces.'

'Shall we tell her Dave or leave it until later?'

'Later Paul, after that greeting we got, in the meantime Miss, I will have steak and chips with a side salad if you please.'

'Make mine the same Miss.'

Throwing back her head she hurried away.

'Do you think we upset her?'

Paul laughed, 'I expect so, just you wait until later, you are going to have a good tongue-lashing, or I miss my guess.'

Jean came back to lay the table looking quite miffed, not saying a word. She finished the laying the table and went off without her usual skip, her nose in the air.

'Oh my dear chap, you have upset her, I do believe you had better get her some flowers for tonight.'

Having finished their dinner, and as Jean was clearing the table, Dave said, 'See you later when you finish work, or are you going home first?'

Jean looked at him, tossing her head. 'I will think about it.'

Looking miserable, Dave got up from the table saying 'I will get us another drink.'

A while later they saw the girls making their way to them, neither of them looking very happy, as they reached the table they sat down without their usual greeting.

Paul asked them, 'What do you girls want to drink?'

'What have you been saying to my friend? You have really upset her, you upset her and you upset me. We want an apology from you both.'

Dave stammered, 'We were only teasing, we were in good spirits and we have a surprise to show you.'

Paul interrupted, 'Now don't you let on what the surprise is, go and get the drinks in Dave, the usual for the girls I think.'

'Well you thought wrong, we will have a drink later when we know what the surprise is, then we might have a drink. That is, if we think it is worth it.'

'OK. Come on Dave, let's go.'

The girls followed them out as they walked up to the car. Turning to them Dave said, 'Fancy a ride out somewhere?' They were both grinning from ear to ear.

'Is this yours Paul?' asked Kath.'

'No, it belongs to both of us, we bought it together and share it. We went to Leeds this afternoon to fetch it, now we can all go for rides out to wherever you girls fancy, so where would you like to go?'

'Anywhere, let's just get in and drive.'

'We can go for a short ride somewhere, we only have about an hour before it gets dark, then we will not be able to see anything. Let's make an early start in the morning, we can get the map out when we come back and pick somewhere. How about it, all agreed?'

They all got into the car laughing and pushing each other. They decided to go on through the village taking the opposite way from Leeds, the boys having never been past the village.

Kath said, 'I have never had a boyfriend who had a car before. I like it not having to rely on buses, you will have to teach me to drive.'

'And you can teach me,' said Jean to Dave who was sat in the back seat with her.

'Shall I tell them our news Kath? Well, my parents have invited you to tea on Sunday Dave, Kath's want to meet Paul as well, that is if it is alright with you both.'

'I did not expect it to be so soon.'

'Don't worry Dave they will love you. Daddy wants to meet you to give you the once-over. He's never met a young man from Leeds, or as he put it a city boy. You will like him and I am sure he will like you.'

'I hope so, I have never been invited to meet a girl's parents before, I am not looking forward to it either.'

'I am looking forward to it, I will have an idea what my future wife is going to look like in years to come, when I see her mother, right Kath?' said Paul, giving a hearty laugh.

'Oh dear, maybe it is not such a good idea.'

'We had better head back now, I don't want to be driving around country lanes in the dark, I will turn around at the next chance.'

Later, pulling into the hotel car park they decided to for a walk.

'Dave, Kath and I will take a walk into the countryside, we will meet you back in the hotel later for a drink.'

'OK. See you later.'

As Paul and Kath walked off, Dave suggested that they went to the park. Squeezing his arm Jean nodded, saying it was a good idea. When they got to the fork in the park Dave said. 'Let us take the side Paul and Kath usually take, I want to see the lake he talks about.'

When they got to the lake they sat down on the grass, their feet inches from the water, looking out over the lake. Jean caught hold of his hand.

'Look the moon is just coming up, it looks as if it is coming out of the lake. This is romantic, we will have change sides the next time we all come.'

She put her arm back though his, he turned to face her.

'It is nice here, we will have to change places. Not that I have any complaints about our spot.'

He lay on his back looking up at the sky, as Jean laid herself on top of him, running her hands through his hair and kissing him firmly on his lips. When their lips parted he rolled her over onto her back, and kissed her again, this time moving his hand over her breasts. Undoing the buttons on her blouse he fondled them, teasing her left nipple until it got hard and then moving to the right one. Their lips parted as Jean give a little gasp. She sat up as, undoing the rest of the buttons, he removed her blouse. His hand searched for the fastening of her bra. Jean give a little laugh.

'Silly, it undoes at the front, let me.'

Jean slipped it off, laying down again as Dave first kissed

one then the other nipple, causing Jean to gasp with pleasure. Meanwhile Dave's hand moved up her leg and around her thighs. Pulling on the top of her panties, he slipped them down over her legs getting her foot caught them, at last he managed to free them. Lifting up her skirt, he kissed her belly moving his lips from one side to the other, then moved back to her neck, his right hand moving down her belly until he touched the mount.

Meanwhile Paul and Kath had settled down well off the path, and were lying down behind a low laurel bush. Paul was saying, 'I never in my wildest dreams expected to find you on my holidays, specially here in a little village, way out in the wilds.'

'What do you mean, way out here in the wilds, what did you expect to find?'

'Not the girl of my dreams that would want to be my wife, to be with always, forever.'

'When I saw you in the hotel from the kitchen door, it never entered my head that I would fall in love with you, you were just a date that Jean had fixed up. That reminds me I will have to thank her for that.'

'When you waved to me in the hotel I thought you looked cute with your red hair, and you were just a date for me then. Who would have thought it would be love at first sight, at least it was for me. On top of that your lifelong friend and mine would fall in love as well. I guess it must what they call fate. I do love you Kath, I meant it when I said I wanted to spend the rest of my life with you.'

'I love you too, and I want to be your wife for ever and ever, Kiss me.'

Paul rolled over on top of her as her lips parted slightly, they kissed long and hard. Her hand grasped his, and pushed it under her dress to her breast. He caressed it, and finding her firm nipple began to squeeze it gently. Putting her hands behind his head Kath gave him an extra hard kiss, then pushing him off her she sat up unbuttoning her dress and pulling it over her head showing her red undies. With a twinkle in her eyes she undid her bra, and as she lay down Paul kissed her nipples, then ran his lips down her belly and back to the nipples. Meanwhile Kath was struggling to undo his trouser belt, and with his free hand Paul completed it, at the same time pulling the zip down. Sitting up he pulled the trousers off, and as he started to pull his pants down Kath said, 'Let me.'

As they slipped down his legs she gasped, 'Oh my, it's hard.'

Paul was busy pulling her panties down. Once off, he pulled her on top of him.

Later back in their hotel room Paul said, 'Well it is our big day tomorrow Dave, we meet the parents, hopefully our future in-laws. Bloody hell, before we came here I had never even thought it, now I am happy to say it, it must be love.'

'I feel the same, except I am not feeling as calm as you about it. What if they don't take to me and put Jean off?'

'You have nothing to worry about. Anyway if Jean loves you as much as I think she does, how her parents feel will not matter. That is how I feel about Kath, we love one another and no one will stand in our way, not even my parents. Look, it is not the time to start worrying, we will know by this time tomorrow, let's try and get some sleep.'

They both jumped into their beds but were still talking an hour later, before they both dropped off to sleep.

Next morning as they had just finished their breakfast the girls came in.

'Look what the wind has blown in Dave.'

'Less of that Mr Talbot or we may just turn around and go,' said Kath with a laugh as she leaned over and kissed him. 'We will both have a coffee if you please gentlemen.'

Not to be outdone Jean gave Dave a kiss on the cheek. 'Well big boy what are we going to do today? You have only got today and tomorrow before you go home.'

Dave shrugged. 'I thought it might be a good idea to see

some more of the capsule, that is if you girls want to. It may be a while before you can see it again.'

Jean, looking at Kath, said, 'We both want to see more of it naturally, but we both decided as we have the full day off to do something else, like going for a romantic drive somewhere.'

'If that is what you girls want, who are we to argue? Right Paul?'

The waiter came with their coffee, they all talked about the meeting of the parents that evening, but not for long because they were all keen to go out.

They drove deeper into the dales, stopping at the falls and other beauty spots, having lunch at a country pub and calling into a cafe they found in one village where they had cream cakes, after they had finished their tea.

'I think we should check the map Paul, we have been driving for hours and we have to be back for tea, or else.'

Back in the car they got the map out, checking where they were. Paul said, 'It will take us about an hour and a half I reckon to get back. It is three o'clock now so we should be heading back Dave, we will want time to smarten up before we enter the lions' den.'

Kath, giving him a gentle punch on his arm said, 'Less of the lions' den if you don't mind, that is my home you are talking about.'

With that Paul, who was driving, started the car and they were off.

They got back to the village at quarter past four. After dropping the girls off they made their way back to the hotel. In their room they both had a shower then dressed with very little being said until they were both ready, when Paul with his hand on the doorknob said, 'Shall we have a quick drink in the bar first?'

CHAPTER II

Future In-Laws

Going quickly to the bar Dave and Paul both had a whisky. Finishing it, Dave put his hand in his pocket.

'Do you want a mint Paul? It will take the smell of the whisky away.'

'Thanks, good thinking, let's go. We can't put it off now, and we had better not be late today of all days.'

They arrived at Kath's house first. There Paul turned to Dave without a word being said and shook his hand.

As Paul opened the gate Kath came running up to him, giving him a light kiss on the cheek. 'You are as nervous as my Mum.'

With Kath leading the way they walked though the hall into the living room where her Mum and Dad were both standing in front of the fireplace.

Pulling Paul by the hand she led him over to them. 'Mum, Dad, I would like you to meet Paul.'

They shook hands, Paul noticing his grip was good and firm.

'It's a pleasure meeting you Mrs Williams, and you Mr Williams.'

'The lad has manners Wendy. Come, sit down with Kath on the sofa while I get us a drink. Kath told me you like a whisky now and then.'

'You have asked him if he wants a whisky, he may prefer tea.'

'Don't be silly Wendy, he must be as nervous as me, and I need a real drink.'

Giving a big smile and a wink at Paul, Mr Williams poured out two good helpings of whisky, giving Paul one.

'To happy times to you both.'

'To happy times Sir.' Paul, raising his glass to them all in turn, drank their health.

'Well then, I believe you come from Leeds. Never did like it, all those people rushing around as if the end of the world was coming, We like the quiet life, slow and easy, don't we love?'

He put his arm around his wife. She pushed him away with a laugh saying, 'What will the lad think of us?'

'I think you are lovely people. Now I know where Kath gets her good looks from, and her nice disposition.'

'That was a nice thing to say Paul. Tell us about your family, have you any brothers or sisters?'

'No Mrs Williams, just myself and my parents, they keep telling me, one of me was enough.'

They all laughed as Mrs Williams said, 'I am sure that is not true.'

They sat talking for quite a while, Paul telling them about his work, how one day he hoped to be manager of his own bank and Mrs Williams telling him about Kath as a child and showing him the family album. They all laughed a lot at some of the photos. As they closed the album Mrs Williams got up.

'It is time I got the tea ready. It won't be long, come and give me a hand Kath.'

When they had gone Mr Williams turned to Paul. 'Would you like another drink Paul?'

'No thank you, I only have a strong drink occasionally.'

'No, I rarely touch it either except on special occasions like today. You are the first lad Kath has introduced us to, it looks like you must be special and I am glad to say I approve, you seem to have won Wendy over as well. Oh, that's Mrs Williams. Yes I think she likes you too, so you are off to a good start, but you treat her right young man.'

'On that you have no need to worry Sir, I have never met a girl like her. My parents will love her like I do, and I want them to meet her as soon as possible. My Mum will be over the moon when she knows I have found the girl of my dreams, sorry, I am not usually so soppy with my words.'

'I was probably just the same when I first meet Wendy's parents, so think nothing of it. Come on, they must be ready for us by now.'

Leading the way Mr Williams took Paul into the front room, where Kath placed him at the table and going round to the other side sat opposite him. Paul smiled at her.

'I like your parents, they are great.'

'Yes, I told you so.'

As her parents sat down at the table her mother said 'Come on Paul, help yourself,' pushing a plate of mixed sandwiches towards him.

It was an enjoyable meal with small talk and happy banter. Later when they went back into the living room, Kath's dad gave Paul a glass of beer which he was thankful for, not wanting to make a fool of himself with whisky. After about an hour Kath got up saying, 'Come on Paul I fancy a walk.'

'OK. I could do with one to walk off my tea, I ate too much but it was all so nice. Thank you again Mrs Williams I enjoyed it, and you Mr Williams,' he said as he shook his hand. 'I hope I can come again.'

They both said that he would be welcome at any time.

Kath, holding Paul by the hand, led him out of the house and in the lane she put her arm through his.

'That was not too bad was it? And they liked you, did you notice Dad giving me the thumbs-up sign as we came out? You certainly got his approval, and you won Mum over, she told me while we were getting tea ready. It has been a wonderful day.'

Turning in front of him she kissed him on both cheeks.

'Is that all I get?'

'For now. I wonder how Dave is getting on with Jean's parents? Her mum will like him but her dad thinks she is too good for any lad, I do hope it all goes well for them.'

Some time later as Paul was making his way to the bar in the hotel, Dave came rushing up to him almost shouting. 'I am in! I got on great with her parents, I am coming to see them again in a couple of weeks.'

'Hold it while I get a drink first.'

With Dave following, Paul got to the bar and getting the drinks, made his way to an empty table near the window. Sitting down he pulled Dave into the next chair.

'Alright, I am all ears and I gather everything went well, so tell me.'

'It was great. Mr Brown, her dad was a bit cool for a while. I kept thinking he didn't like me but after a couple of beers, and a barrage of questions, he suddenly leaned over and shook my hand saying, "You are alright for a city lad." After that it was great, they could not have been nicer. You should have seen the meal, chicken and salad with home-made cakes. By the way Jean had made the cakes so she is a good cook. How did you get on with Kath's parents?'

'Like you, great. I really took to them and I think they did to me.'

They stayed until the bar closed. Finishing off his drink Paul got up.

'Come on let's go, we have both heard in detail how we made out, how much we both impressed them, we hope. Let's go to bed, I am ready for mine.'

'Yes, and let us think of something special for tomorrow. It will be our last day and the girls said they have the afternoon off.'

The following morning at breakfast they asked the girls what they would like to do.

Jean said they had already discussed it and had decided, that is, if they agreed.

'Well out with it girl. Dave and I have things to do.'

'Although we have lived here all our lives we have not seen

much of the dales, and you having a car we can all go exploring. It will be fun, after all that is what you came here for, so let's all do it together.'

'That's a good idea, as a matter of fact, it is a great idea. What about it Paul?'

'Seeing that was why we came in the first place, yes. Can we get a picnic basket made up by the hotel?'

'I will arrange it.'

As Jean started to go Paul said, 'Make it for four people and a bottle of red and white wine, and we will meet in the bar at two.'

'Make it two-thirty, we will need to go home and change first.'

'OK. Two-thirty it is, now run along, Dave and I have things to do.'

Giving a smile and a wave with her fingers she was off among the tables.

At two thirty-five the girls came up to the bar a bit out of breath.

Paul, winked at Dave, who said, 'Girls you are late, and why are you panting?'

Kath give him a gentle push. 'You are impossible, why Jean puts up with you I don't know.'

'She loves me.'

Dave gave Jean a quick kiss.

'Let's go or the day will have gone, and I will carry the picnic basket.'

They made their way to the car laughing and pushing each other to hurry along.

They spent the afternoon driving in and out of tiny villages, getting lost a few times ending up at field gates. While having their picnic on a hill overlooking a valley, they watched a couple in a small boat in the river below.

Jean said in a dreamy voice as she lay down, 'What a wonderful day, and to think this has been on our doorstep all this time, Kath. Look what we have been missing, we must come again, lots and lots of times.'

Turning, Jean pulled Dave to her and give him a kiss, then another.

'We will come again, say yes, Dave.'

'Of that you can be sure, whenever we can and we will make this our favourite place.'

Kath looked at Paul. 'Jean is right, it is lovely here and we must come again.'

Later as Paul looked at his watch, he said, 'Do realise we have been here for over two hours, if we want to see more we should think about moving.'

'Come on Kath we will take a look around, the boys can put the picnic things away.'

'Just like women leave us to do the work, and stop calling us boys, right Dave?'

'Stop calling us girls,' called back Jean.

Minutes later Dave called them back.

'We are ready when you are. Come on, or we can pick you up on the way back if you like.'

Kath and Jean came running back, both throwing their arms around them saying as one, 'You just dare leave us that's all.'

They kissed, and laughing, got into the car.

A couple of hours later as they were driving into another valley, they drove into a small village with a pub called 'The Sailor Inn.'

Paul pulled up outside it.

'Let's stop here for a drink, I want find out why an inn so far from the sea should be called 'The Sailor Inn'.

As they got out of the car Jean called out, 'Last one in buys the drinks.'

Dave laughed, running to catch up to the girls.

'Paul called back, 'That's not fair, I have to lock up.'

However when Paul got to the bar Dave had got the drinks in.

Picking up his drink Paul asked the landlord about the name of the inn, since they were a long way from the sea.

'I wish I had a pint for every time I have been asked that. You see it was like this; over a hundred years ago it was called the 'Dog and Duck,' but a new landlord took it over and renamed it, "The Sailor Inn". The story goes that his only son was a sailor, so that was why.'

After having a couple of half pints each, it was decided they would make their way back to the hotel. They got back just in time to order a dinner since by now they were all hungry.

When the meal was over, with much talk, mainly by the girls concerning how much they had enjoyed the day, and some drinks later, the girls said it was time for them to go home. They had the early shift, and they wanted to sound out their parents. It was the first time either of them had taken a boyfriend home.

'We will leave you here and walk home by ourselves tonight, see you in the morning.'

Paul and Dave kissed them goodnight and with a wave they were gone, linking arms as they walked up the road.

'I will call in to say goodnight to your parents on the way home Jean. I want to find out what they thought of Dave, and to tell them about Paul,' said Kath.

Meanwhile Dave and Paul had sat back down at the table with fresh drinks.

'I want to take Jean to meet my parents as soon as possible. What about you and Kath, we may as well arrange to do it together. You know I will not be able to keep it a secret from my Mum for long, she will know something is up the moment she looks at me.'

'We can both tell them as soon as possible, and let us arrange for them to meet in two weeks. If the girls agree, we can ask them tomorrow. Wow, I can just see Mum's face, she will not believe I am serious about a girl, at last. Dad will just say, "About time too".'

'I would like to take Jean home with us when we go now, I know we can't, but it would be great. I still find it hard to believe we found two girls who are as close friends as we are, and we all fell in love, the odds must be thousands to one.'

'We can ask the girls, but it may be a good idea if we met our parents all together, you with yours and I with mine for a meal. That way the girls can meet both families, I am sure the girls will like it better that way. What do you think?'

'Yes, a good idea, we can put it to them tomorrow.'

'Come Dave, let's finish our drinks, we can have an early night, we have had plenty of late ones lately.'

Next morning Dave sat up in bed, looking at the clock, then throwing a pillow at Paul, called out, 'Wake up there, it is eight o'clock, breakfast finishes at nine and the girls will be wondering where we are. I will have first shower this morning for a change, get yourself up.'

Paul opened one eye looking at Dave. 'Why did you have to wake me up now? I was having a great dream, and it was just getting interesting.'

'By my deduction, it must have been Kath you were dreaming about.'

'I don't know, it was her body that not her face I remember. Come to think of it may have been Jean I was dreaming about.'

With that, Dave took a running dive at Paul landing on top of him, laughing and holding his fist in his face.

'If don't keep your eyes off Jean, even in your dreams, this is what you will get.'

They both rolled off the bed. Paul, jumping up first, ran to the bathroom, slammed the door shut and locked it, calling out.

'Thanks, I guess I am still first, better luck next time mate.'

'Some mate you are.'

Running down the stairs they barged into the dining room, then walked quickly to their table as Jean followed them.

'What time do you call this? We have just about finished

with breakfast, actually I believe we have.'

Dave put his hands together as in praying. 'Now is that the way to treat your future husband? If this is what I can expect, I may have think again.'

'Alright, but this is blackmail, What is it to be, a full English for you both? Come on, or it will be too late.'

CHAPTER 12

The Stag Night

Paul and Dave were called into the manager's office. On the way Dave looked at Paul. 'What do you think he wants us for? I hope we are not on the carpet for anything, I've made no mistakes that I know of, have you?'

'Not that I can think, we will soon know.'

Paul knocked on the door.

'After you Dave.'

As they stood in front of the manager's desk, he got up with his hand outstretched.

'I have not congratulated you both on your forthcoming marriages. Next Saturday, I believe. You are both the first members of my staff to tie the knot as it were. What arrangements have you made for your stag night? I take it you are going to have one.'

'Yes, we have been talking about one, we just haven't decided on anything yet, have we Dave?'

'Good, then with your permission I would like to. I will arrange everything, just leave it to me, what about next Friday?'

Dave and Paul looked at one another, both nodding their agreement.

'Thank you both, you will not be disappointed I can assure you.'

Thanking him again they went back to their posts.

Tim, who was working next to Dave, whispered 'Well what was all that about, you in trouble?'

'No, he wants to organise our stag night,' Dave replied.

'Oh God, what have you done? I was looking forward to a fun night.'

'We had to say yes, I like my job here, it will be OK,' whispered Dave.

By lunchtime everyone knew. They all thought the same as Tim, leaving Paul and Dave feeling confused, not knowing whether to risk telling the manager someone else was going to do it. Talking it over they decided to make the best of it.

They had been informed by a notice on the board, that the stag night was going to be held in the bank's social hall, starting at 7 p.m. on the coming Friday.

The girls thought the manager wanting to arrange it all was a good sign.

Dave and Paul wanted to know, 'A sign of what?'

The girls just laughed. 'We are having our hen night in the hotel, and on our boss.'

Paul and Dave arrived at the club early at 6.30 p.m. Walking in the door they were surprised, there was a four-piece band on the stage getting set up, balloons and bunting everywhere. In the far corner there was a bar being set up, with crates of beer and wine.

'Paul, Mr Godwin has done us proud, he said to leave it to him. Wait until the lads see this, we will not be calling him an old stick-in-the-mud again,' Dave said with a grin.

'Who would have thought it of him? This is great, we will have to thank him,' Paul replied, putting his arm on Dave's shoulder.

Then they heard him behind them. 'Well lads, what do you think, do you like it so far? There is more to come. This is the first stag party I have arranged, I am sure everything has been covered for a good night.'

'Mr Godwin, you have done us proud, thank you, it all looks great.'

'Well don't just stand there, your guests are arriving, go and greet them.'

Paul and Dave rushed back to the door, then it was non-stop for them, as their guests appeared to come as in groups. Many of them had bottles of wine with them, Dave and Paul told them to take them to the bar.

'Dave, I did not know there would be so many. It looks like Mr Godwin has invited people from other banks, I recognised some of them from other branches.'

It was at eight-thirty when Godwin, who had gone onto the stage called for silence, and asked for two chairs to be put in front of the stage. This was done with him placing them well apart, then picking up the microphone he called to Paul and Dave to sit in them, which their friends with plenty of ribbing escorted them to.

On Godwin's wave the band give a drum roll. When they stopped he held up his arms for quiet.

'Now for your entertainment, let me introduce Sergeant Petite and Dolly Got It.'

Another drum roll as the girls danced their way towards Dave and Paul. Sergeant Petite wriggled and vamped her way to Paul, Dolly Got It did the same to Dave, holding a mask in her hand over her face as she danced up to him.

There were many shouts of 'Get Them Off' as they gyrated in front of Dave and Paul, then the girls changed places, Dolly Got It slid up to Paul, still holding the mask to her face, Paul had his hands over his eyes, then she sat on his lap moving her ample breasts with the nipples brushing his fingers. Paul not knowing quite what was going on, took his hands quickly away from his face knocking the mask away from hers. He sat there open-mouthed looking into her eyes.

'Monica – what the – ?'

She leaned over his ear whispering, 'Please, don't say anything, you never saw me before.'

Then she carried on dancing and swaying in front of him and just before she finished her act she whispered, 'Come to the dressing room in a few minutes.'

After a lot of ribbing from their friends, as everyone settled down to dancing or drinking again, Paul managed to find his way to the dressing room. When he knocked on the door it was opened by Monica, and pulling him in she gave him a kiss.

'That's for not letting on you knew me. Sit down, I want to explain.'

Holding up his hand, Paul said, 'You don't have to explain anything to me.'

'I want to, but first how have you been, are you getting on well at the bank? It has been a long time, now you are getting married. Congratulations, and Dave as well, a double wedding. That is why I am doing this job, it is only a night one, I am still working during the day as an accountant's secretary. I am engaged to be married in three months' time. My fiancé would have a shock if he knew I did this. I only do it in other towns away from him, we need the money to pay for everything, my Dad can't help us much. You won't tell anyone will you?'

'Of course not, congratulations to you as well. Fancy us meeting again like this, it was a hell of a surprise. I saw more of you tonight than I ever did when we went out together, you looked great,' said Paul, smiling.

'Stop it, you will make me blush in a minute.'

They both laughed as she pushed him out of the door.

Saying goodbye he walked back to the hall, grinning to himself, muttering, 'Would you believe it?'

Dave came over to him with a beer. 'What have you been up to, nothing good by the grin you have.'

'Tell you later.'

It was midnight when Godwin managed to stagger onto the stage, picking up the microphone.

'Before we call it a night, let us all give three cheers to our guests of honour Paul and Dave, wishing them well and good fortune for tomorrow, their wedding day.'

With that both Paul and Dave were picked up, put onto someone's shoulders and carried around the room, everyone cheering and drinking their health.

Later back in their bedroom, Dave said, 'Paul, fancy old Godwin getting the girls. Boy that was a turn up for the books, what a night, by the way what was that Dolly what's it, whispering to you?'

'Oh, it was nothing.'

'Come on, I saw the shock on your face. Did she make an indecent proposal, come on out with it.'

'If you must know, I knew her. Remember my eighteenth birthday; the girl I was with was Monica, she is "Dolly Got It". You remember I stopped seeing her because she moved away with her parents. Anyway keep it to yourself. Now goodnight, get some sleep. It's our big day tomorrow and we don't want to upset the girls, do we?'

Saturday morning 7 a.m., the telephone rang.

'Shut that noise up Dave, the phone is next to you.'

In a sleepy voice Dave answered it, 'Hello.'

'Your early morning call, Sir.'

'Thank you.'

'It was only the early morning call, now let me get some sleep.'

A few minutes later he sat up with a start. 'Paul, wake up. We are getting married, or have you forgotten?'

Jumping out of bed he rushed over to Paul, pulling his bedclothes off him.

'Stop it, my head is about to explode, stop shouting, I heard you the first time – Oh my God, what time is it? I am getting married this morning. Oh! my head. Ring down for some black coffee and some pain killers, please Dave, or I will never make it.'

'I told you not to mix your drinks, but, oh no, you knew best.'

'Shut up and get the coffee. Leave me alone, tell Kath I can't make it,' moaned Paul.

'Oh no you don't, move it.'

Then there was a knock at the door.

'Tell whoever it is to go away, we don't want any.'

Dave opened the door, just enough to see who was there.

'Come in fellows. It is our best men, Paul.'

'Well come in, but quietly, and get my coffee Dave.'

Tim said he would go for some. Paul staggered to the bathroom, putting his head under the cold water.

'Whoo, ha! It is damn cold.'

Minutes later he came out drying his hair.

'That feels better, just a cup of coffee, I will be OK.'

It was not long before Tim came back with a steaming jug of coffee and four mugs.

'I got mugs, hope that is alright.'

Tim put the tray down and poured them all a mug-ful each.

After they had drunk about half their coffee, Tim looked at Jack saying, 'Right, I will make a start. Come on Paul you first. Into the shower with you while Jack and I sort your clothes out. Come on move it, as best man I have to get you to the church on time. Jack you look after Dave.'

By half past eight they were dressed and ready, buttonholes pinned to their jackets.

'We have done a good job Tim, now for some breakfast.'

'Not me boys, my stomach couldn't take it,' said Paul.

'Just have a doughnut and coffee, you had better have something inside of you.'

Paul rolled his eyes. 'Let me have another coffee first.'

At nine the waiter came over to them.

'Your taxi has arrived, Sirs.'

'Come on Paul, we had better be moving. How are you feeling now?'

'Not as bad, that coffee helped. Remind me never to have another stag party.'

Tim put his hand under his arm lifting him up. 'Come on, we don't want to keep the girls waiting.'

'I can manage to get up myself, thank you.'

Paul stood up holding his hands above his head. 'There, look no hands.' he said, grinning around at them.

'I am not drunk, just feel bloody awful, I must have got the daddy of all hangovers. I'm ready let's go. How does that song go Tim, "Get Me To The Church On Time"? That's your job, off we go,' laughed Paul.

They all laughed as they made their way to the door and getting into the taxi they were all feeling more relaxed.

Getting out of the taxi, Dave looked at the crowd standing outside the church.

'Wow, Paul, I bet there would not have been half as many people, had we been getting married in Leeds. I'm glad the girls decided on their home town.'

With Jack and Tim leading the way they went into church. It was packed with family and friends on the girls' side and their side was well packed with their family, but they were surprised by the number of friends that had come from Leeds. Their bank manager was there with his wife and two sons and it looked like the rest of the bank staff were as well.

Dave and Paul stood side by side in front of the altar, with their best men beside them, until the vicar rearranged their position, telling them to make room for the brides.

Dave whispered to Jack. 'You, I will not have you for my best man again.'

'I hope you are not planning another wedding already.'

'Shut up, you idiot,' said Dave, giving Jack a push.

Then the organ started to play. They all turned around to look at the brides as they walked down the aisle, Kath in front with her Dad, followed by Jean and her Dad. Coming up to Paul and Dave they took their places beside them.

The vicar called a number for a hymn. As it was being sung Paul whispered, 'You look lovely, out of this world.'

'Quiet,' said Kath, trying to look serious, and smiling at the same time.

The hymn finished and the vicar waved for the congregation to sit.

'We are gathered here to witness the marriage of two young couples, David and Jean, Paul and Kathleen. This is my first double wedding, which I am honoured to perform. I have known Jean and Kathleen since they were young girls, when they both attended our Sunday school. I will now read the wedding service as for one couple, except for the vows.'

When the time came for their vows, both girls lifted up their veils, both turning to face their men to make them. As they finished, the vicar said, 'You may kiss your brides now.'

Paul gave Kath a short tender kiss, and turning his head he looked at Dave, who was kissing Jean as if there was no one else around.

'You can stop now Dave.'

Dave stopped, looking around blushing like a young boy stealing his first kiss. Another hymn was sung as they followed the vicar to the vestry. When everyone had signed the register, the vicar leading the way, they lined up to walk back down the aisle, this time it was Jean leading.

Dave gave Jean a gentle squeeze with his arm. 'You look like an angel.'

Reaching up she kissed him lightly on the cheek, then they were outside, the photographer pulling the couples together, taking a few photos of them in different poses, then taking them as separate couples. There were photos of one group after another until at last he was finished. Then it was the turn of the family and friends, shaking hands with kisses and congratulations. Finally, the best men took them to their individual cars, which were to take them to the reception at the hotel. As the cars drew up at the hotel, their manager was there, a large bouquet of flowers in each hand, one for each couple.

Kissing both girls on the cheek he shook hands with Paul and Dave.

'Congratulations, there is champagne on your top table, compliments of the hotel.'

Paul and Kath, Dave and Jean stood at the entrance of the

dining room, both girls looking radiant in their brilliant white gowns and still holding their bouquets of red and white roses, having let the matrons of honour take the bouquets from the hotel.

First came their parents to kiss and congratulate them, Mums with tears in their eyes saying how lovely they looked, and for the next half hour they stood at the doorway, receiving kisses and handshakes, passing their presents to their best men, who placed them on tables they had positioned just inside the door. There were so many that they had to put some under the tables.

Then it was time to go to sit down, and since it was a double wedding, two top tables had arranged, the wedding cakes placed on small tables in front each of them. The hotel had brought in extra waitresses, and were soon busy putting plates of salad in front of everyone. It was an hour and half before the meal was finished. When the tables were cleared, the best men both stood up together, asking all to stand and rise their glasses to toast the brides and grooms, then the bridesmaids.

Then the fathers gave their speeches, both letting some little secrets come to light about their little girls. It was the best men who let the grooms' secrets out, causing quite a few laughs and cheers. When the speeches were over the best men read out the cards, including quite a few cheeky ones, causing more laughs and cheers.

Later after the brides and grooms had made their rounds of the guests, introducing each other to friends and family not previously met, it was time for them to go on their honeymoons. Coming down from their rooms after they had changed into their going away outfits and running the gauntlet of their friends to their cars, the girls turned and threw their bouquets, causing excited whoops from the girls that caught them.

At the car Paul turned and shouted, 'No, and we are not going to the same place for our honeymoons.'

The cars drove away with cheers and tears, amid the banging of the tin cans tied to their bumpers.

CHAPTER 13

The New Beginning

'My name is Samuel, I am the great, great, great grandson of Joseph. Thousands of years have past since the last entry, this is the only capsule with this entry in it in which we hoped to record how our civilisation was rebuilt.

'For the first few hundred years good progress was made and basic towns and villages were rebuilt mainly with the robots. Then as the robots and the sleighs failed, towns and villages fought each other. Those who were badly organised raided others who were better off than themselves, and this became commonplace across the planet. It was at this time that the planet leaders and scientists got together, and decided they would have to separate themselves from the general masses, hoping to be able to lead the people back to civilisation. It would take a lot of planning, how and where to start. After much deliberation, it was decided to all gather in the place you call Britain, which was the least populated area and an island, with a moderate climate. With no sleighs workable over the rest of the planet, except for those that we had stored, we could be safe to plan how we could influence the people in the right direction. It took time for all the leaders and scientists to gather from all around the planet.

'Our first task was to organise the growth of food. Here we had willing help from the local inhabitants, which were few in number. Towns were built and generators were set up to supply electric for lighting and computers, which we had kept stored in the pyramids. With careful maintenance we could expect them to last a long time.

'After many years our island became self-sustaining; we were even able to build workshops to repair and maintain our equipment. We still could not replace the robots or sleighs but we could keep them working. We had continued to survey the planet, and found that all the different races had divided into hundreds of groups or tribes who fought with each other, over food, land or because they all had their own gods.

'It was decided to send the men in ones and twos, to infiltrate their own races, with their own languages. Many of these became known as wise men and were able to influence the leaders of the tribes they were with. Gradually tribes began to blend together and formed nations, religions began to become as one with the different races, so there became fewer gods, although there were still different gods which were worshipped for the wind, rain, love and war.

'The land known as Egypt still had many pyramids. These were suggested as tombs for their pharaohs, many of them were used as such, which then became symbolised as tombs. It had been the practice to be buried in the place that became known as the Valley of the Kings. Some of the Sphinx had lost their animal heads during the conflict with the Ords so the pharaohs had their stonemasons fashion new ones in their own images.

'The men that had gone to the west to help the Mayas, and later the Incas to built large cities, to develop their horticulture and develop a great civilisation. It took hundreds of years; men we had sent out did help, but as they died, so did the climb back towards our planet's former greatness.

'The downfall of the Inca civilisation started with the invasion of their empire by the Europeans, who demanded gold and a change of their religion. Then they started to migrate to the land you call North America and, over the years they spread across the continent, separating into tribes and developing their own religions. You know them as Red Indians. Similar events took place in Europe, it separated into different counties, China followed a similar pattern.

What the final outcome will be only you will know, as this may be our final record, good luck to you all.'

CHAPTER 14

The Professors

'Hurry up Paul, Dave and his family will be here shortly. I told you to get dressed before you put the drinks out,' said Kath, as she brushed her hair and finished dressing.

Paul came in, looking smart in his new casuals.

'David and family are in the garden, I can hear the twins, I hope they behave themselves this time. I will call them in, as you said Dave's lot should be here soon.'

Then they heard a car come up the drive and they both ran to the door. Kath got there first, and with her hand on the doorknob turned to Paul.

'Is my hair alright? I forgot to look.'

'Don't worry, you look just fine as always.'

Opening the door they were greeted by hugs and kisses from Mary, who turned to the young boy and girl who were just behind her.

'You remember Joe and Linda. Come on you two, give Uncle Paul and Auntie Kath a hug, are Mum and Dad here yet?'

'No, Jean rang me to say they were on the way.'

They both gave Linda a kiss on the cheek, Joe holding out his hand to shake Paul's.

'Well you are growing to be quite a young man now,' Kath said, as he solemnly shook Joe's hand.

'Go on in while I give your mum and dad a lift with the luggage,' laughed Paul.

Going over to the car Paul gave Mary a hug and kiss.

'You are as beautiful as always.'

'Stop flirting with my wife and give me a hand,' said James.

'Here James you can take these two big cases of yours.'

Facing Paul he caught hold of his hand and hugged him.

'How is everything Paul? Are you still having problems with your boss at your branch? Anyway you have only six months to go, then you will be retiring, Dad will be following you next year. Here give me the suitcases, we will talk later.'

Picking them up James led the way into the house.

'Leave them here in the hall for now, we can take them upstairs later. David and his family are in the garden, not forgetting the grandchildren, look out here they come.'

'Look out, here come the terrible twins, my terrible grandchildren who are the apple of my eye. As you will remember this one is Robert and this quiet-looking one is Steve, don't forget, quiet in looks only.'

Ruffling their hair, Paul said 'Say hello to your auntie and uncle then.'

They both gave Dave and Jean a kiss and a big hug.

Robert turned to Steve saying, 'We will have some fun now that granddad is here. Come on, Steve let's go in the garden.

'I suppose we may as well, and leave the grown ups to talk.'

They went running out into the garden.

'Come on you two, let's get a drink while you give us your news. Look out here come my offspring,' said Paul moving James to one side.

Coming into the garden were Paul and Kath's children, David and Margaret.

Paul put his arm around Dave's shoulder as he led him into the lounge, Kath had her arm through Jean's as they followed them.

'Where is David?' said James looking around for them.

'They were in the garden with the children, I thought. I will have a look.'

As he got to the patio he turned. 'It's alright, they are coming.'

Paul walked back in followed by David and Mary who said 'Sorry about being out when you got here, we went for a walk for some peace and quiet from the children. That is what we like when we come here, it is so quiet walking down the lane with only the birds singing. We do love it here.'

They all kissed and shook hands, all saying how nice it was to be together again.

With a glass of wine in their hands they all sat down.

'My, I like your new suite Kath, have you had it long?' asked Mary.

'It only came two days ago, Paul brought it for our anniversary, I was worried it would not arrive before you, we could do without that hassle when we have guests.'

'It is lovely, but who would have thought it, that we would both be celebrating our fortieth wedding anniversary together, and been friends all this time.'

Paul looked at Dave and Jean.

'It is not just our anniversary today, this is the day that we decide what we are going to do with the time capsule, but let us wait until the children are in bed. Can I top anyone up?'

Later when they had their dinner, the grandchildren having gone off to the bedrooms to unpack their cases, the washing up done and put away, they had all gone out into the garden to sit down, the men had brought the wine and the glasses to the tables.

Paul raised his glass, 'Health and happiness to us all, may we celebrate many more anniversaries together.'

They raised their glasses, as they sipped their wine, and toasted each other to many more.

Paul looked around.

'Now, shall we decide what we are going to do about the time capsule? We have a video each, Dave and I; we have also got a more modern one each that we took two years ago. Now that we can do hologram videos it is just like the original. Any ideas?'

'Well I have been thinking,' said Dave. 'One of my clients at the bank is a Professor Gibson who is on the government science committee. I am on friendly terms with him and we often have a drink together. We could invite him to join us one weekend to have a look at it; there could not be a more appropriate time, now that it is in the paper about that historian saying it is strongly thought that there was a pre-civilisation, thousands of years before ours. They are even saying it may have been millions of years before ours. Well, what do you all think, or is there a better idea from anyone?'

We have kept to ourselves too long, but we can't keep it quiet forever,' said Paul. 'I think we should let Dave contact the professor he knows, everyone agree?'

'That sounds like a brilliant idea,' they all agreed.

We can make it another family get-together if you are all up for it, or I can come on my own Dave,' Paul continued. 'Well, what shall it be? You know the man Dave, think he would mind meeting us altogether the first time, or just you and me?'

'Let me sound him out, see how he will feel about it, I am sure he would be interested,' said Dave. 'When do you think we should arrange it for? Shall we say a month's time, or thereabouts?'

'You say if and when, Dave, we will leave it to you. Well, that was soon sorted and here I was thinking it would take us hours to decide. Now we can hear all the family news, I am sure you ladies will be more interested in that.'

'I am glad it was sorted so quickly before the children came, I know we will have to tell them before it becomes common knowledge. That's if it does of course, what do you think Paul?' said Dave with his hand on Paul's shoulder.

'I agree we will keep it from them for the time being, see what this Professor Gibson will say about it,' said Paul. 'Meanwhile I would like to see it again myself. I know James and David have not seen it yet. How about you Dave?' Paul looked around at them all.

'Yes, it would do us all some good to see it all again, but let us wait to see what arrangements we can make with Professor Gibson, it should be possible for us to arrange to see it all together;' said Dave. He snapped his fingers. 'I have another idea, there is a small hall not far from us which is used as a sports changing room, I should be able to borrow or hire that. Leave it to me, then if we decide to let the children see it at the same time there will be plenty of room, the ladies can make some refreshments because it is a long programme, and we will need a break.'

'That is good thinking and a good idea, let's leave it for now, we are getting those looks from the ladies. Alright, the subject is closed, your turn ladies,' laughed Paul.

Kath looked at Paul. 'About time, but it was good timing on your part because here come the children.'

First came Steve with a football, running up to Dave. 'Are you going to have a game with us granddad, you promised.'

'Yes' said Dave. 'Come on fellows, who is going to be on whose side?'

Paul went up to Robert and Steve tossing a coin.

'Heads Robert has first pick, tails Steve, here goes.'

He tossed the coin.

'Tails it is. Steve has first choice,' said Paul picking up the coin.

Steve shouted, 'Granddad you are on my side.'

'What about me?' called Jean, 'I want a game.'

With that all the women came onto the lawn saying they all wanted a game.

Three-quarters of an hour later the girls were sitting on the grass saying they had enough. 'Who won?' asked Jean.

'We did' shouted Steve, 'Five goals to three.'

Everyone joined them on the grass laughing, saying that was fun, as the men sat down together.

'It is no good Paul, you are getting too old.'

David patted him on the shoulder. 'Well Dad you can't be young for ever, you didn't do bad for a granddad.'

They all laughed; after a while the children got bored sitting around so they went to play on the swings.

Kath shouted to all, 'Who would like a glass of lemonade?'

There was a consensus of approval from all, as Kath and Jean went into the house, coming out shortly after with trays of soft drinks, lemonade, raspberry and coke. Putting it on the table they called out, 'Come and get it, what do you all want?'

The children all grabbed a coke each, the men saying they all wanted coke as well. Jean pretended to glare at them, saying 'That is it. You men are all the same, there is only one left and I am going to have that, so if you want one you can go and fetch it, they are in the cool box in the kitchen.'

'Don't worry. Come on Dave, give me a hand, I know where the beers are. David, James, fancy a beer?' asked Paul.

They all got up and trooped into the kitchen with Paul going to the fridge. He got two four-packs of beer out, then went into the lounge.

'That's better,' said Dave, falling onto the sofa.

A few days later as they were getting ready to leave, all agreed that it had been a great little holiday and that they would have to do it again, and more often.

Paul was saying that even the boys must have enjoyed it, and at least they had behaved themselves.

'We will leave it to you to contact Professor Gibson, let us know how it turns out with him.'

Shaking Dave's hand Paul turned to Jean. 'I have shaken your husband's hand now I can kiss his wife. Come here and give me a hug. It has been great Jean, I expect we will be coming up to see you shortly when we meet Gibson. Come on kids give your uncle a hug and look after your mum and dad. Well James and Mary it has been great seeing you both again. Take care; we will see you again shortly.'

As the cars drove away there was a lot of waving and blowing kisses until they were out sight.

Five weeks later on the Friday night everyone met again at Dave's house, that is except for Mary and James' family. They planned to be over in the morning as they only lived a few miles up the road.

After they had all settled down and the children had gone to bed, Dave said, 'Paul, as I told you over the phone, Professor Gibson is coming to that hall that I have booked for ten in the morning. As you know I told him a little about what we had and he will be fetching a colleague with him, will that be alright with you?'

'Of course it will, he will be able to back Gibson up if anything comes of it. Did he say anything about this colleague of his,' asked Paul.

'No, only that he carries a lot of influence on the committee, which may be a good thing. Well at least after all these years, we are going to find out if we did the right thing in keeping it to ourselves.'

'What about you David? You are keeping very quiet, cat got your tongue? Come on, let's have some input from you. What about a top up, and you Dave, your glass needs it and how about you ladies? Can your drinks stand freshening up?'

'I will have a top up Dad, it is a lovely wine, it has a sweet bouquet and taste,' said Mary.

'Hark at her, a sweet bouquet, we have a connoisseur among us,' laughed James.

'Quiet James, you are only jealous because I have a taste for wines, anyway blame my Dad he was always telling me to know my wines.'

'There my fault again. You try to do the right thing by your children, then it is your fault,' said Dave.

'Only kidding Dad,' she said blowing him a kiss.

David turned to Paul, 'I will not be able to give much input about your time capsule, I have not seen yet. Dad only told me a few days ago, a very short summary about it, sounded far-fetched to me, but I will reserve judgement until I see it for myself.'

'Fair enough, but you are in for an interesting time, or maybe I should say, shocking.'

After a lot of small talk Kath said, 'It is gone eleven, time for my bed. Are you coming Paul?'

'I guess I am, and I won't take much rocking tonight, can hardly keep my eyes open so I will say good night too.'

They all got up saying they were all ready for bed as well.

As they all trooped off to bed Jean started to pick up the glasses, Dave giving her a helping hand.

'I will just wash these glasses. You go up Dave I will be along shortly.'

'OK, but only the glasses.'

The following morning at eight o'clock, they had just finished clearing up after breakfast, Dave called out, 'Everyone help with the food hampers and take them out to the cars.'

Jean told the children to fetch some bats and balls, or anything else they might want to play with.

Meanwhile Paul and Dave went upstairs and came down carrying a big bag between them.

'We will put it in your car Paul, my boot is already full.'

As they were getting into the cars, Dave went to James' car, 'Can you take this hamper and box with the drinks and things in the boot of your car, we will take the food with us. Paul has got the capsule and video.'

It was quarter past nine when they got to the hall. While the children went to play ball on the field, the adults arranged the table and the chairs, Paul setting up the time capsule.

As they had finished and checking everything looked alright and in place, a voice from the door said,

'Can we come in?'

Turning Dave saw Professor Gibson standing there with a big man, almost twice as big as the professor, walking over to him.

'I am glad you could make it, Professor,' he said, shaking his hand.

'This my colleague, Professor Poole who specialises in ancient history, this is Dave Carter.'

Leading them both to the group, he introduced them all in turn.

Paul said, 'I hope you will not mind but we have brought our children with us, they have not seen any of this, they will be quiet, but if they are not we will let them play outside.'

'By all means, it is your show if that is the right word, come let us sit down.'

Paul called the children in but they preferred to play in the field.

Dave, who was at the other side of the capsule, explained what they were going to see, first showing them the capsule and how it opened then closing it again. He explained that they would be seeing a hologram, but a video of it had been made for them to take away. 'Now if you are ready, we can begin,' he added. There was a lot of oh's and ah's from the children. The professors looked as though they were going to say something a number of times, however, they reluctantly remained quiet until it finished.

While the women prepared the refreshments, the men got together in a group. Dave asked the professors what they thought of it. Professor Poole spoke first.

'I wonder if you would mind if Professor Gibson and I discuss it in private, just for a while, this is a very interesting find.'

'Not at all, we will go and join the women, I am sure they could do with some help.'

The two of them went to the women and as they got to them Jean said, 'Everything alright? I see you have left the professors on their own.'

'It's alright. They want to talk about it on their own for a while. Look at them, they certainly appear to be excited about it.'

When the refreshments were all laid out ready, the children having helped themselves to sandwiches and drinks, Kath, who was handing out the drinks called to Paul.

'What about the professors, shall I ask them to come over?'

As they looked they were walking towards them and as they reached the table Kath smiled at them.

'I was just thinking of coming over for you. Now what would you like to drink? There is tea, coffee also soft drinks, and help yourselves to sandwiches and cakes.'

They both smiled at her. 'We will have coffee please, just a cake for now, we don't want to spoil our dinner.'

'Dave said you may like some refreshments, also you may have questions to ask.'

Professor Gibson looked at Dave, 'What we have seen is incredible, it is going to revolutionise history. What will it do to the archaeologists? There have been so many theories about the pyramids, Stonehenge and so many other happenings; the explanation of why there are four races on our world, why that alone will cause problems. Europeans will not take kindly to it, nor will anyone else except the black races. What do you think Professor Poole?'

'This will have to be seen by our full committee, by all our members from around the world. I do not think any of you should discuss what you have seen on this capsule and what ever you do, you must not let a word of this get into the newspapers. At this moment in time, I cannot see if the world will ever be ready for this kind of news, can you, Professor?'

'Oh dear, you are right, but my, there are some colleagues I would like to shoot down in flames. I can just see their faces when they see this, of course they are going to pooh pooh the idea.'

We will have to take your copy with us, then at some later time if you would both come to London, all expenses paid of course, fetching your time capsule and letting our members see the original. It will take very careful handling before it can be made public, it maybe be years before we can do that. Well can we take it with us, then study it fully in our own time? We need to take notes as we go along. We will need to authenticate it as much as possible, also to date it, quite a task in itself,' Gibson said, looking at Poole.

Paul looked at Dave and nodded, 'Yes, we think that would be a good idea, you will keep us informed with your findings of course.'

Kath and the rest of the women went out to see how the children were. 'Hope they have been behaving themselves, we did tell them not to come back until we are called.'

Jean called them and they all came laughing and skipping to her. 'I see you all appear to have been enjoying yourselves.'

They all went back inside, the children helping themselves to more drinks and cakes.

Meanwhile, Dave led James aside. 'Well now that you have seen it, what is your opinion of it?'

'Dad, the thought that hit me first was, "Is Orion Home?" I mean the planets of the Orion Belt, are they the home of our ancestors? This is going to shock the world, here we have been wondering for years, are there any other intelligent forms life out there, now we find out that we came from the stars.'

'James, that is something I had not thought of, or any of us I think. Come, let us ask the others.'

Going over to the group who were talking to the professors.

'Listen everyone, James just told me something incredible. Go on, tell them what you said to me.'

James repeated what he had said.

Gibson and Poole looked at him.

'Good heavens Poole, the boy is right.'

That started everyone off, an hour later they were still talking, until Gibson looked at his watch. 'It is getting late, we have quite a journey in front of us, and I hate driving in the dark.

'Yes, we must be going,' agreed Professor Poole.

Poole shook first Dave's hand then Paul's.

'It is truly incredible, incredible, remarkable, when our colleagues see this, their worlds will collapse.'

Throwing his hands above his head, he repeated, 'Collapse

I tell you.'

Turning to Gibson, Poole grasped his hand in both his and shook it so hard Gibson winced.

'Come on Paul,' said Dave. 'Let them talk on their own for a while, we could not get a word in anyway, look at them, like two schoolboys.'

Later after the professors had left, Paul laughed. 'Did you see the way Professor Poole was hugging the tape machine, it is a pity they don't have that model. As Gibson said it is a bit out of date, but he will be able to transfer it to one of theirs. Poole is not going to part with that easily. I do not think Professor Gibson liked it, he had to drive leaving Poole to carry it, I wonder which of them will be looking after it?'

'At least we can let some one else worry about it now.'

'Come on we had better help getting everything packed in the cars.'

Paul walked up to the two women. 'Alright girls we have come to help. What do you need us to do?'

'Now that is typical of men, Jean. "Can we help you?" Now that we have done everything, even the children are in the cars. Men!' said Kath with her arms in the air.

Back home with the children all in bed, they were sitting in the lounge with a glass of wine.

'Well Dave, I guess we got the professors' interest.'

'They were like two schoolboys, I wonder which one of them will be looking after the machine and tape tonight, that was a good thought of James about our ancestors. It appears that we did come from the stars, well done James.'

'I guess it was a fresh mind, and seeing it all through for the first time, what a turn-up for the books, I am glad the young ones did not see it today, can you imagine them keeping quiet during a history lesson, they would be telling the teachers they had it all wrong, we could be called in to school, then what would we say?'

'A good point, thank goodness they wanted to play instead.'

After a couple of hours discussing the day's events, quite a few glasses later it was decided to call it day and go to bed.

As they got up, Paul said, 'Things will never be the same for the professors again.'

Dave, with his hand on Paul's shoulder, replied, 'When it is made public the world will never be the same, let alone the professors. There will be one question; "Is Orion Home?"'